EDITED BY A.C. BAUER

CAT EYE PRESS

To Mom

TABLE OF CONTENTS

INTRODUCTION 9
A.C. Bauer

FRANKIE'S INTRODUCTION 11
Frankie the Cat

BOUND BY LOVE 13
Stewart Moore

GOING HOME 28
Ute Orgassa

OUR HEARTS A HECATOMB 36
J.R. Santos

DEAD KINGS, NO CROWNS 48
Christopher La Vigna

#RICH-TOK 60
B.F. Vega

ONE HUNDRED DEAD CATS 73
Kristin Dearborn

REANIMATION 91
Carter Lappin

PAINTED AS A VILLAIN 101
Morgan West-Burnham

IN MY LITTLE, DEAD WAY 113
Jennifer Lesh Fleck

ROT 130
Ray DeChant

THE TELLTALE LVAD.................................150
Meg Candelaria
SERVANTS OF FROST AND MADNESS.............161
Zach Shephard
BY THE WORLD FORGOT................................177
Mia Dalia
ABOUT THE AUTHORS 191
ABOUT THE EDITOR(S) 196
CONTENT WARNINGS 197

INTRODUCTION
A.C. BAUER

've been interested in mummies ever since I was a kid. Not strictly in an academic sense, though. No, it was more in a "this stuff is kind of scary and I love it" sort of way.

I remember playing a terrifying little game called "Mummy" at my babysitter's growing up. One of the older kids would wrap themselves up tight in a bed sheet and lie in wait for the perfect moment to attack us younger kids. The game was pretty basic. If the mummy "got" you, that was it. Game over. It was simple, but I remember screaming and having a lot of fun with that one.

I was haunted by the *Goosebumps* cover illustrated by Tim Jacobus of a mummy with glowing red eyes. If you've seen that cover, you know how those eyes just seemed to stare right into your soul.

I also spent time being scared by the "1999 cinematic classic" *The Mummy* staring Brendan Fraser and Rachel Weisz. I even dabbled with some of *The Mummy* TV series on VHS (man, do I feel old saying that).

Truth be told, I even think the first "real" scary story I ever wrote was about a mummy. It was in third grade and the mummy was part balloon, but it was for a Halloween assignment, so I think it counts.

Safe to say, the mummy archetype has been with me forever it seems, which makes sense given that mummies have basically been around forever too. Mummies are iconic. They're enduring characters in the horror genre.

I think part of that endurance has to do with the nature of death itself. Death is this big scary thing, the punchline at the end of a lot of horror. It's a great, inevitable unknown that awaits all of us. Death is one of my greatest fears (for better or for worse), and to overcome it would be… well, I don't know. I'm sure it'd be interesting at least.

And maybe that's some of what makes mummies interesting too. What choices would they make after they've come back to life? How would they react to getting a new start in a new time and place? Would they be happy? Upset? Would the state of our modern world impress or depress them?

Questions like these, along with the desire to expand the scope of what mummy horror can be, motivated the creation of this anthology. I hope you enjoy the answers we found.

FRANKIE'S INTRODUCTION

FRANKIE THE CAT

Hiya, folks. My name is Frankie and I'm the handsome fella on the cover of the book you're reading. I'm also the brains of Cat Eye Press, no matter what A.C. says. I see myself as an integral part of Cat Eye Press, a co-editor/co-owner/co-captain if you will, so I wanted to share some of my own thoughts about this project.

So, why an anthology on mummies?

Well, as A.C. said in his introduction, mummies are fun. They're iconic. And they're kind of underdogs when it comes to the pantheon of classic monsters. Vampires and werewolves have been done time and time again, but mummies? They seemed a little harder to pull off. So, we thought, why not give it a shot? Why not breathe some new life into the mummy genre?

Because the fact is, mummy stories have kinda been stuck in a rut. Many follow the same old mummy tropes (revenge, reincarnation, reincarnation *and* revenge, etc.) and downplay the mummy as nothing more than a shambling silent villain. We wanted to provide an opportunity to change some of that.

Inside this anthology, you'll find the mummy reinvented and reinterpreted for a modern world. You'll find mummies from far beyond the confines of ancient

Egypt. You'll find stories of unusually well-preserved bodies that challenge the notion that mummies have to be wrapped in bandages (although I will say, it's quite the fashion statement and one that I pulled off nicely). You also find mummies beyond just human mummies (cat lovers be warned) and in all shapes and sizes.

These are modern mummies. They run the gamut from ancient mummies operating in the modern world to mummies being created in the here and now.

It's gonna be fun, so why keep you in suspense any longer? Go on, start reading!

BOUND BY LOVE

STEWART MOORE

The cancer ate Simon as we hate-watched season three of *Ancient Aliens*. His money and insurance ran out long ago. Friends, virtual and otherwise, lost touch as he drifted away. His family made their feelings clear the one time I tried to call them. His doctors probably assumed he was dead. I was all he had left: his sort-of landlord, the owner of this creaky, drafty old house that once had been my parents'. I'd sat by their bed in their last illnesses. I knew what to do now.

"Kathy," he whispered, his voice hardly passing further than his pillow.

I muted a man with odd hair who claimed the pyramids were a secret alien sex farm. "I'm here," I said. "I'm not going anywhere." I'd said the same thing to my father and then my mother. I was even sitting in the same chair.

He murmured something. I leaned closer.

"I want you… to mummify me." It took him two breaths to say it, and three more for me to understand it.

"You're crazy."

"I'm dying. I'm more sane… than ever." He poked me with a skeletal finger.

"It's got to be illegal. A health code violation at least."

"My body… my choice."

I turned off the show. "You're not serious."

Simon grinned. It was a ghastly expression on his gaunt face. "C'mon, Kathy. You have a Ph.D… in Egyptology… and you work… in a Starbucks. Don't you want… to put your degree… to use?"

"I never had to mummify anyone in graduate school." Maybe if I had, I would have gotten a job as a professor. But probably not.

"Still…" His smile stretched his face taut. "You know how."

I didn't, of course. I mean, I knew where to make the incision into the side to pull out the organs, and I knew basically where the organs were. I knew the body had to rest in natron for forty days, but I couldn't remember exactly what natron was made of.

I pulled out my phone. Maybe it was curiosity. Maybe it was because in the end, I couldn't say no to him. But in five minutes, between Wikipedia and Amazon, I knew how to make natron, and how much it would cost. Not that much, really.

Simon's eyes gleamed, the only luminous things in his ashen face. "You know you can."

He was in agony. He needed to go. I gripped his hand, a jumble of bones in my fingers. "Tell me why you want this."

He gathered strength and spoke with more breath than I'd heard him use in a month. "When my parents disowned me, they said I'd go to Hell."

"You don't believe that."

Simon shook his head. "But if they're going to Heaven, I don't want to go there either. I want another option. All the times you talked about Egypt, death there… just sounds better. I want to walk in the Field of Reeds. I want to weigh my heart against a feather. I will be judged there. I will be justified." He sighed and closed his eyes. It took almost a minute before I was sure he was still breathing.

Simon was my boarder. My roommate. My friend, and somehow, in his illness, we were the family we no longer had. I thought about him leaving me, maybe tonight. I thought about standing over his bed, his corpse. I thought about calling 911 and letting some strangers take him out of my life forever. I'd done that twice already. I'd scattered my parents' ashes by the ocean where they met. Gone from me. All gone.

Something in the shadows in the corners shifted, some quality of the light or of the dark. Simon was mine. He didn't belong to health agencies and bureaucrats and hospitals. He was mine. And I knew I couldn't call 911 a third time.

"Okay," I said.

He smiled. He never opened his eyes again.

I made my first orders that night.

No Egyptian text records the prayers the embalmers are supposed to say as they work. If I'd believed anyone was listening, I would have been worried. But this was between Simon and me. If Anubis cared, he could keep it to himself.

I carried Simon's body to his bathroom. He was so much heavier than he looked, as if the greedy earth wanted to pull him into itself. No. Mine. I hefted him into the tub.

I washed off the sweat that the effort of dying had left crusted over his skin. I was pretty sure his hair would fall out during the embalming, but I shampooed it anyway.

The next step was to remove the internal organs before they digested themselves. I carried his naked body downstairs to the basement and laid it on my father's old worktable. The operation is supposed to be done with an "Ethiopian blade." No one knows what that means, so I told the kitchen knives they were Ethiopian and that would have to do. I laid down a tarp. I kissed Simon on the forehead. I took a breath.

You make the slit on the left side of the abdomen. I pressed the tip of the blade to his cold, fragile skin. This was the last moment before I committed a crime. The last moment before a process began that would last seventy days. The last moment this ordinary-looking house in an ordinary neighborhood would be nothing more than what it seemed.

I cut. Thick blood welled over the blade, and my house became the House of the Dead.

The rest of the night was a blur. I remember my arm up to my shoulder in Simon's thorax, hacking blindly at the connections between his organs, pulling out shamefully butchered chunks, covering myself with blood and bile and shit. I gagged and vomited and wept and apologized to him over and over for my clumsy hands. For the first time, I knew why the embalmer who cut open a corpse was beaten and cursed by the others. I was violating Simon. But this was what he wanted. I knew, in the end, that he and I were in this together.

I put the organs in trash bags and packed them into the refrigerator, to preserve individually later. His shrunken frame looked truly skeletal now, the loose skin sinking into the empty belly. But his heart still lay in his chest. Or what I guessed was his heart.

He was beautiful. He was mine. And I was his.

At least it was winter. At least there wouldn't be flies. I turned on the dehumidifier. This wasn't Egypt, but I would do what I could.

A bird sang, a cardinal, the first one of the morning. The sky outside the basement window was deep blue. I had just enough time to clean myself off before my shift started. The smell of ground coffee was like the smell of ancient spices. Dazed by exhaustion and what I'd done, I spelled customers' names with especial creativity that day, but everyone got what they ordered. Eventually.

My own packages began arriving. A little pyramid waited for me on my front step. When I opened the door, an astringent smell of spoiled meat greeted me. I ordered air fresheners and took my stuff downstairs.

Simon waited patiently for me. I made myself as cold and hard as the hammer and thin chisel in my hands. I broke a hole through the back of his right sinus. I stabbed the blade into his skull over and over, reducing his brain to fragments.

The Egyptians believed the soul lived in the heart, not the brain. I had to trust they were right. Simon wanted this. I told myself that over and over.

I pulled the bits out with a hook I'd found among specialty cookware. The brains were viscous and clung to the hook. I put the pieces into a mason jar. All his thoughts, his memories, his funny sayings: they flew free with his *ba* and would come home to his body. I knew this. I made myself know it.

By the end, my hook scraped the inside of the skull. I'd done well. I had to admit I wanted this, too.

Something scratched at the window. I looked up into the face of a black dog about the size of a beagle, with sunken, hungry cheeks. It whined and clawed at the glass. When I turned my back on it, it barked. I washed my hands and checked my phone. Two a.m. I couldn't have a dog bringing attention to the House of the Dead in the middle of the night.

In our kitchen, the only thing remotely doggish was a can of beef stew. I poured it into a bowl and went outside. The cold gripped my bare arms. I went around the house to the window where the dog had been, in the backyard.

It sat on the porch, panting its breath into smoke on the air. Its ribs cast shadows on its chest. It twitched with every step I took toward it, but it didn't run. When I put my foot on the first stair, it stood and barked. I leaned forward and put the bowl on the porch, then backed away. Not until I'd walked around the corner did I hear the snarfling of food.

The dog didn't bark for the rest of the night.

The next day, huge bags of baking soda, table salt, sodium carbonate, and sodium sulfate arrived: the ingredients of natron. Simon would rest in that white powder for forty days, drying out and preserving him. Egyptologists debated whether the corpse lay in a bath or a huge jar. I decided on a contractor's bag. It was undignified, but since I was mummifying Simon in much lower temperatures than in Egypt, I figured I needed to maximize the contact of skin and salt.

Muscling the corpse into the natron-filled bag was awkward. Rigor mortis had mostly passed, but gravity resisted me at every turn. The Egyptian embalmers worked in teams, so dignity was easy for them. Anubis would have to settle for what I could manage alone. It was a heavy, sweaty job, but at least not a long one. Once Simon was in the bag, and I'd thoroughly cleaned the basement, the air fresheners started to get ahead of the smell of putrefaction.

Not enough for the dog, though. It scratched and whined again that night. I'd planned for this and had dog food aplenty. I set out a bowl on the porch, and I hardly slid the door closed before he came and gobbled it up. No barking that night, and I had my first decent sleep since Simon died. Now I just had forty days to wait.

The dog kept coming back, no matter how much I thought I cleaned up the last of the corpse odor. I checked lost pet sites but no one near me was missing a black dog. After a week, I had to feed it both in the evening and the morning to keep it quiet. Simon had always wanted a dog. I always said no. I was too tired to remember why.

But Simon would never leave me now. He was transforming. His bag swelled with gases released from his body. Without the organs, it wasn't as bad as it could have been, but I still watched the expanding black balloon with unease.

It finally split on the thirtieth day. The stench that erupted when I opened the door was otherworldly. The air fresheners were like sandcastles melting in a high tide. I finally understood why embalming was done on the west side of the Nile, while everyone else lived on the east. Ancient cities smelled mostly like shit, but at least shit didn't smell like this. I barely made it to the bathroom before puking.

Once I was only dry-heaving occasionally, I pulled Simon's half-desiccated, eerily light body from the bag. His slimy corpse clung to me, and I to him. It was like a premature birth. And this part of Simon's journey wasn't over yet. I wrestled him into a new bag with what natron I could mix from the leftover salts.

The old bag slopped with an awful pinkish-brown sludge. I tied up the ends of the tear, then put that bag into a succession of three more bags. What I would do with that bundle of joy, I had no idea.

The dog started barking. I couldn't do anything about it until I cleaned off. I rushed through a shower, terrified the doorbell would ring, and the police would tell me to quiet my dog—and then they'd smell a dead body. They would take Simon away from me. They'd tell me I was crazy, and all sorts of wrong things. I yanked on some clothes.

The dog stood in my backyard and glared at me, its eyes mirroring the porch light. But at least it stopped barking. It looked healthier now, its chest fuller.

I'd prepared for this moment. I set down my new cage trap and put the dog food inside. The dog ran once in a circle then stood and stared and whined. I backed up into my house, closed the door, turned out the indoor lights, and sat in the shadows where I could watch the cage.

Nothing happened for a long time, at least that I could see. Sometimes the dog barked again. For a moment, my thoughts lashed out and wished the poor thing would drop dead. I had to protect Simon. I couldn't let a stray dog reveal our secret.

The cage clanged shut. Terrified yipping cut through the night. I grabbed my keys and ran outside. I hefted up the cage, snarls, hackles and all, and shoved it in the back of my car.

I drove a long way. My hands trembled on the wheel, and I drifted side to side in my lane. The constant barking drilled into my brainpan. "I'm sorry," I kept saying, "but they'll take him away from me if you don't stop." I drove until I was over the Delaware River into Pennsylvania. I pulled over by a park and let the dog out. It could bark at me all it liked now, but it didn't. It stared at me, judging and whining. I opened the cage. The dog growled. I walked backward, in case it tried to attack. It never did. It lay down in the cage and gazed up at me through the open door. I got in my car and drove away.

I had a six a.m. open the next day. I've never been so tired in my life, and it's possible some people never got their orders. But once I got home, the air fresheners had taken the edge off the corpse juice smell. At least a little bit. I tried to sleep, but all I dreamed of was a black dog barking.

I counted down the remaining days, a fog of making coffee and obsessively checking Simon's bag for holes. I painted hieroglyphic spells in red paint on the plastic to keep it sealed. Packages arrived for the next phase. And then the ten days were over.

With a mask over my face, I opened the bag. No stench seeped through. I dared to breathe in the air. Simon smelled like beef jerky now, sweet and a little tangy. I pulled him free and carried him easily to the bathtub where I washed him inside and out. His joints were stiff but could still be pressed into new positions. I laid him back out on the workbench.

No one knew the exact combination of spices the embalmers used. My best guess was incense, cloves, and cinnamon. The House of the Dead smelled like a cannabis pumpkin pie. I dared to put the bags of natron and juice out for the garbage collectors. God bless them, they took the refuse away. Simon didn't need that stuff anymore.

The next step was wrapping. The embalmers used thirty days to do this. I assumed this was because they kept stopping to say prayers. Since I didn't know the prayers, I thought it would go quickly. How wrong I was.

Though Simon was light, wrapping each finger, toe, arm, and leg separately was tricky. The linen bandages came loose if I didn't tie them up, but tying them up made a lumpy mummy. I started over twice. The day came when I would see his face for the last time. I kissed him goodbye and wrapped his head.

After bandaging each individual limb, I had to wrap his whole body like a cocoon in strips six inches wide. I would lift him up gently, pass the roll of linen under him, tug it secure and then do it again. It was so much harder than I thought. Again I wished for more embalmers who could give this rite the solemnity it deserved. But Simon worked with me as best he could, tipping easily from one side to the other. We were joined together by our work, by his body, by his magical, wonderful mummy.

I finished with three days to spare. The last thing I did was bind a flash drive with a copy of *The Book of Going Forth by Day*, vulgarly known as the Book of the Dead, to his chest. He would need to know the name of every demon and doorpost in the Netherworld to reach the judgment hall of Osiris.

Of course, there's no such thing.

I sat on the floor and looked up at my work, at my dear one. The cream-colored linen looked like it had come fresh out of a sarcophagus. My brother embalmers might not have been uncritical, but… maybe grudgingly impressed. Simon could stand tall among his fellow dead.

At the cliff's edge of exhaustion, I picked him up and carried him upstairs to his room. My proud tears soaked dark circles in his bandages. Wrapped head to toe, he was stiff as a board. I had to maneuver him around corners like a stick of furniture, apologizing the whole way. I laid him on his bed. He hardly made a dent.

I had wondered, now and then, what I would do with a mummy in my house. At this point, Simon would outlive me by far. But that was a problem for another time. I slept the sleep of the justified.

—

Midnight. The seventy-first day. I woke up. I'd heard a noise. But what? I cleared away the shreds of dreaming to find the hard reality that had pulled me awake.

The dog barked. My whole body went cold. The barking went on and on, a complaint raised to whatever gods and neighbors were listening. But that wasn't the noise that woke me up.

Thump.

The next room.

Thump.

Simon's room.

Thump thump.

The dog howled.

I got out of bed, so tired I didn't care if the Eater of the Dead waited for me with lion claws and crocodile teeth. I staggered to the hallway. I opened the door.

Simon lay on the floor, his wrapped body flexing at the hips then slamming down again. I stared at the miracle, too exhausted to comprehend.

Someone pounded on the front door four times, paused, then pounded again. The police, surely. I closed my eyes and gathered what few threads of strength I had left. The police would hear Simon's thumping and think someone was signaling for help. I turned on an action movie and cranked the volume. I went downstairs, eyes shut, trailing my fingers on the wall to guide me. I opened the door and squinted into the night.

Not a cop. Just some guy in a robe. "Would you let your dog inside, lady? He's waking up the whole neighborhood. At this point, frankly, I don't care if he craps on your rug. One more bark and I'm calling the cops."

Once he finished his rehearsed speech, I mumbled an apology and stumbled past him to the walkway.

The dog sat on the spring-damp grass, dark eyes gazing into mine.

"Okay," I sighed. "Come here, Anubis!" The name seemed obvious in retrospect. "Come on! Come inside!"

Anubis jumped up, barked once, happily, and ran past us into the house. Despite his threat, my neighbor only spared me one last glare, then padded off in his slippers. I closed the front door behind me.

Anubis was nowhere to be seen. My breath froze. I ran upstairs.

He sat in Simon's doorway, watching the mummy twitch. Images of canine teeth savaging those carefully wrapped bandages dissipated, but dumb shock at the impossibility of it all held me fast for long moments.

Scissors. My numb heart came to life. I needed scissors. Down the stairs, up the stairs. I had to sit on Simon's writhing body to hold him still. I hacked away at the outer layers that bound his arms and legs and covered his head. Finally he bloomed from the exploded wrappings.

Astride him, I looked down into his desiccated features, the face I thought I'd never see again, the face of a thousand years. The eyes had dried out to raisins in the sockets, the lids sunken in. Still, they opened in tiny jerks like curtains rising on a midnight show. Darkness stared into me.

Simon's teeth chattered. No, not chattered. They clicked together, trying to form words. No air moved inside his body, but I heard the ghost of his voice, his spirit, his *ba*. I muted the movie and leaned my ear in until his dry lips brushed them.

"Kathy… There was no one there. I had the book, I knew the names, but no one was there. The gates, the mounds, the caverns… all empty. Nothing spoke. No one on the throne of Osiris. No one holding the feather of Ma'at. No one to judge me. No one to care. Where did they go? Where were they?"

I got off Simon and lifted him onto the bed. He'd been to the Netherworld and come back. It was real. It was all real, all along. But was it possible for a whole afterlife to die? For gods to pass beyond after thousands of years without worship?

Or was it me? Was it that I didn't believe, that I didn't know the prayers, that I said nothing the whole time— nothing to anyone who might listen?

"I don't know, Simon," I said. I sat in my chair. Gravity settled on me as if I would never rise again.

"It was horrible. Horrible."

"Yes. It must have been."

Anubis trotted in, hopped up on the bed, and curled up at Simon's feet. I remembered then why I always told Simon we couldn't have a dog. Because someday Simon would leave me, and then we'd have to fight over who kept the poor thing.

But Simon would never leave me now.

"You can stay here," I murmured. "I'm not going anywhere." What else was there to say?

I put on *Ancient Aliens*, season four.

Anubis grunted in his sleep.

GOING HOME
UTE ORGASSA

I am dead, but I'm alive. I have clung to my body despite my expiration. I am a ghost in a shell. Not really a shell, mind you. The bog preserved me, innards and all. My face, frozen. My skin, leathery and darker, so much darker than it used to be. Running away from a beast, I stumbled, fell and got sucked in, sucked under. Did fear kill me first, before the water? It is possible. Remembering is difficult. It has been eons. It just happened. Ghosts don't do time well.

Why am I paying attention now? Because they are moving me. They. People, like I used to be, but looking rather different on the outside. The bog released me and now I am officially found. Why can't they leave me be? This is my resting place where I am one with the universe. This is my natural state now. I exist in harmony with everything around me. This is my home. I like it here. There is no need to scrutinize, analyze, prod and compartmentalize any part of me. At least the ghost is still attached to the shell, so I am coming with them when they load my leathery brittleness into some van. That is what they call the huge wagon-like structure that makes infernal roaring noises.

The experience of speed is unsettling and invigorating at the same time. But the loss of home and context and equilibrium makes me angry. I scream my anger at the strangely covered people in the van. They shudder and look panicked. They talk about being a bit spooked. Can they hear me? Could the world always hear me? I never ever tried before. I was content to be quiet. Let nature talk to me and for me. Not now. Rage works itself through me. My silent screams pour forth. They cannot hear me, but it doesn't matter. They can feel the rage. Even my face looks more angry than fearful now. One of the people remarks on that. How it can be interpreted both ways. The other one says that fear is the most likely reason for my grimace, on account of dying in a bog and all. On any other day before I would have agreed with him. But today I am learning new things about myself. One of them being that I still somehow have a semblance of control over my features. It is in equal measure baffling and welcomed.

They bring me into a massive place that is all sharp angles and noise. The doors clang loud like gongs. The contraption they use to wheel me all around squeaks. The place itself is cold and incredibly bright at the same time. No sunlight is warming me, but it is brighter than noon. I can feel the energy of that light. I send some hate its way.

They roll me into some chamber, turn off all the lights and leave me there. I savor the dark, but I feel exposed. There is no bog to hug me. Not another living thing anywhere near me. Everything around me is hard, cold, blank, square. The streamlines of this place permeate my differences. I do not belong here.

I wait. I have no idea for what. But I can't make things happen on my own. I can't get up and walk back to my bog. I want to, but my bones do not follow my commands. I want them to. I concentrate on that. This timeless place has nothing else for me to do, observe, or go through. I spend every instant of my existence on this. It might be hours; it might be months. I make progress. I get to the point where I can move my left index finger. Nothing else, just this. It's a start.

The door opens, the intrusive brightness exists again from one moment to the next and people are gathering around me. One of them speaks, several watch, another applies instruments to my body. They hold things in their hands on which they make tapping noises. They talk with excitement. They leave. I practice in darkness. They return. My existence is now divided into dark loneliness and bright intrusions. They run heavy humming equipment over me that makes me even more angry. I know they don't want to hurt me. They keep warning each other to be careful and to keep me intact. But who gives them the right to disturb me so constantly? To take me away from my peaceful resting place and declare me their property? I certainly did not. I can move my eyes now. Just a little bit.

New people come. More people. They wheel me into a different chamber. I can tell that some of the regulars are there too. The one they call Doctor is talking. The one they call Dan is standing beside me. I stare at him. I focus all my energy on him. He looks back. He changes position. My eyes follow him. I stare at him. His face shows fear. Success! I might be primitive, as Doctor keeps saying, but I know what fear on the face of a man looks like.

They pack me away. I practice in darkness. My left foot can swivel now. It makes me giddy. I wish I could talk. Tell them to take me back. All I can manage is a dry crackling, like a dying fire. I can scream on the inside, my ghostly yells reverberating into my own being, but that still does not make noise on the outside. Speech may be beyond me, but progress is progress.

They are moving me again. And someone notices that my foot is in a different position. People get excited. They come at me with their instruments once more. They go over every inch of my body. They talk about different angles, about measuring mistakes, about theories for change. Dan eyes me with trepidation. I think he knows that I am alive in a way. He does not want to know this. I move my finger. He scrunches his eyes closed. One of the others, Jenna, laughs at him. He does not like that. I can tell. They exit the chamber but leave the lights on. I want my darkness, damn it!

Dan is back. Alone this time. He pulls up a chair and sits right in front of me. He has his tapping tablet and observes, watches, waits. I can easily outwait him. That's what I've been doing. Waiting. Waiting to go home. I stare past him.

But a few moments in, he starts talking to me. Not about me, to me. Nobody has done that since before I died. I like this. Of course, he starts with a lie.

"I'm not scared of you," he says.

I let him talk. I listen. I learn. The shape of his soul becomes visible to me. He leaves too soon. A new idea forms in my consciousness. It will take eternities in the timeless cold box to get myself to move. To sit, to stand, to walk. And even if I manage that, I do not know where I am, nor how to get to where I was. All I know of home is that it is somewhere outside of this prison.

Dan returns. He keeps watch. He repeats the meticulous measurements that have been done before and logged and verified. His numbers don't add up. He calls me Boggy.

"Now what in the world makes you move?" he asks. "There has to be a logical explanation, and I am going to figure it out."

He is determined, stubborn. He is not so different from me. Well, aside from the point that he is actually living. He is how I used to be. Moving, breathing, with a heartbeat and a healthy appetite. He jokes that I better not tell on him when he eats a sandwich in my chamber. I watch him calmly. I am beyond the need for food. I feed on something different instead. His mind. It is open to me. I get to know him and turn his thoughts around. He tells me his secrets and I soak them up. He asks me if he should ask out a girl. I move my right shoulder. Didn't even intend to do it. He yelps. It takes some time before he returns.

I decide to focus on calming his mind when he does. Hate will not get me out of here. I have learned that. I need Dan to trust me. I need Dan's legs to take me places, his hands to carry me. As much as it feels great to have him fear me, it will do nothing to make him cooperate. Let him pity me for all I care, as long as that leads to me getting back into the bog. Where I belong.

His interest in me is not emotional. But I do have his attention. I am a puzzle to him. A thing to figure out. He tells me that he was startled by the suddenness of my movement and that was all. I can still find his pockets of fear. But I agree that his curiosity is much stronger. He spends more time staring at his tablet and tapping on it now than he does looking at me.

I tell his mind that I want to go home. I blast it at him again and again and again and again. I give him visions of my home when he falls asleep. I make him want to go there himself. I work hard on keeping my anger, my frustration away from him. He gets only longing, not the fury of being stuck elsewhere. It is difficult and I scream in frustration when he is not listening and focused on other things. I scream so much; other people avoid my chamber and whisper about strange auras and bad vibes. Let them. I don't need them, I have Dan.

He comes in every day now. That's what he says. I am stuck in this bright, timeless void. I take his word for it. He tells me he has strange dreams. He tells me he has read up about my time, my era, my people, my bog. He tells me that I am special. I implore him that I want to go home. He shakes his head. The bog, I plead. Take me to the bog. He walks around me. Measures my body for the umpteenth time. Something is shifting inside him. He is thinking bog thoughts. I make him feel my longing and his breath hitches.

"This is crazy," he says. "I can't just do that." He finally got my message.

The light goes out. Oh, how I welcome this change! It calms the consciousness, and it lets me rest. Just forget about myself and my predicament. Dream of being home. I send my dreams to Dan and feel his faint response. He dreams about it too. The bog. He wants the same peace, the same calm, the same unity with nature. I am in my chamber. He is close, but does not come and disturb my dreaming. Others are less considerate.

Some of those other people burst into my chamber. And with that, of course, comes the light. They repeat those tired old measurements again. They talk about Dan. They use words like unhinged and obsessed. They laugh about his longing for the bog. I feel offended on his behalf. I send some hate their way. They are too coarse to even perceive it. Brutes, all of them. At least they also turn off the light when they leave. I return to my longing dreams.

Dan comes back. He looks different. There is a spark inside him, a seed awakened, a new form of life, of mind. Determination radiates from him. He gently puts me back into the strange traveling bag. He rolls me through the maze of my prison. He loads me into the roaring van. He speeds away with me. I'm going home. I know it.

When he uncovers me, I feel the bog calling out to me. It feels so right. Home. It is nighttime and I can tell it by the gentle darkness and the sounds of the animals. The air is vibrant, the waters call me. My longing echoes in everything around me.

Dan carries me to my resting place. It is not the one I was taken from, but close enough. He kneels and gently lowers me down. I sink back. Where I belong. Where we belong. I can feel his mind wrapped around mine, bonded forever. I feel his body plunging next to mine. He belongs to me now. He and I will have eternity together.

OUR HEARTS A HECATOMB

J.R. SANTOS

I woke up from my long sleep wearing a jade mask and wrapped with woolen cloths the priests had lovingly wrapped me in.

Anacaona, he called me. I never saw the man before in my life. It was the first of many shocks, though he was even more baffled than I; he hadn't expected me to speak. He jumped back in terror as I lifted myself from my covers, my dissected flesh laid bare for the world to see.

Mother of God! His name was Miguel, and he would have swung at me with an old and much worn macua-huitl—in desperate need of repair—which he grabbed blindingly from a crate, if not for Jacinta.

She was afraid, but unlike Miguel, she had a brave heart and staggered through words familiar to me. I answered, with much faltering, in the mother tongue and felt horror at my own voice. I was surrounded by cargo, these two strangers in clothes I had not even dreamt of before, and not too far away were more of these people, keeping their distance and their silence. So it was I who gave two hesitant steps and nearly fell, my heavy mask almost falling off. Jacinta came to me and held me up, and shielded me from the horror of my face.

The warehouse had other things besides objects of my people; there were cluttered things such as closets and great mirrors, the likes of which I couldn't have dreamt of in my living days. Our mirrors were polished metal or a water's surface. Here was glass, and when I saw myself, I wept.

The mask was beautiful and had some distant likeness to what I had been in life, but the rest of me belonged to the underworld. I gasped audibly and became aware of the dryness of my lungs, the feeling of my withered lips under the mask, how they crawled back to expose my teeth.

It took months to acclimate me to the world, and my second life was kept a secret. I learned Spanish and became increasingly aware of the inventions of the new world, so radically changed from my own.

I would not be allowed to see anything resembling the old ziggurats or the green forests of my childhood. The empire was dead, though the children of the empire carried on living, surviving one hecatomb after another.

Our gods no longer answered our prayers, even though our bravest had offered their hearts at the altars to great honor. I myself had no recollection of my wanderings during that abyss of time.

Perhaps I had been cursed to sleep in my own flesh for some crime long forgotten. If I committed a sin, I beg you believe me: the gods did not reveal my crime to me. I remembered little then of my own death. I dream now, as I tire of the waking world and find myself unable to cope. I sleep—just a couple of hours now and then, but I sleep—and I recall my last day among the living, chased by something monstrous. I recall being torn in a way I had never before been torn, and that I bled more that day than I had ever bled before in all my years. How short they were, those years. I was a grown woman, but still young. I had no children of my own.

I remember I loved, but who or why, I can't recall. It's gone with my own name. I'm Anacaona, now and forever; the goddess can come for me should she wish her name reclaimed. I would happily be taken away.

Even though my existence was hidden, the rumors spread. I was taken from my country, flown and driven in turns across borders that mean nothing to me. I have spent the last forty years in Los Angeles and will likely stay here.

It seems such little time, but in some ways, it was too much too long. Something odd happened, stranger than my second life. All the fantastic things evolved so much faster. I was still listening to music on my Walkman when I was told these black mirror tablets were how everyone interacted with the world now. Obsolete, I was told. The tablet, which they call a phone, though it looks nothing like the ones I had grown used to at the start of my second life, filled me with horror. I could scry into people's most private thoughts; lights flashed and all manners of sounds took to the air to torture me.

I swore them off and remained with my obsolete miracles. But my story is going astray.

Jacinta became my caretaker, and I grew to love her. Her connection to the world I knew was slim, and I felt miserable still, but slightly less so with her. Her hair was long and dark like mine had been, and the birthmark by the corner of her bottom lip drew my eyes to it. A beauty mark, she called it.

We both improved in speaking each other's language, though she spoke three, and learned of each other's worlds. I did not live to see the Spanish come, and after what Jacinta told me, I was glad of it. I wept, tearless, for the bright children taken by sickness and blood-ied hands. Warriors are expected to bleed in battle and die in war, but visions visited upon me were things of a nightmare. Betrayals, hunger, and the befoulment of our homes and temples.

Jacinta wore a crucifix suspended between her breasts.

"Why? It was their god, not ours."

She shook her head sadly.

"It was too long ago. It's been a comfort to me."

What little I understood then was no comfort to me; it seems the followers of this God-child had a sickening obsession withs suffering, shaped by their lust for blood and a desperate need to hate one another. Their great obsession is redemption, and it cannot be gained without first committing a sin. I cannot fathom what sins Jacinta could confess to, but all I tell her is this: when we sought redemption, we did it only once. The gods do not offer second chances.

I despair at the madness of it, but having said my piece, I let go. Is this rebirth not a second chance?

And if every world is destined to the same fate as mine, it will only be a matter of time until they become ghosts, half-remembered and committed to tall tales. Jacinta. She smells of flowers, her hands rest on mine and she feels no disgust at my repugnant touch, breathing hope into my strange existence.

Miguel has a different light in his eye, the madness of gold. He would hold me tighter to him than a mother holding a babe to her breast, for people will pay with blood if they must for the chance to touch a miracle. As thirsty beasts to a river, those who feared death would come to drink of me, for I was hope of something more than darkness upon the veil being lifted from their eyes. Miguel knew this with the instinct of a predator and would drive the herds to me and take his pick, eating his fill of their wealth.

A gathering ensues, then another.

No devices are allowed, Jacinta always by my side, but still, we were doomed.

People ask me questions I can't answer, about death and the meaning of life. They demand my memories of my lost world for themselves, and reel back in disgust when what I provide is not what they wanted. I will not lie, and I can't provide more than what little I have. Still, they accuse me of lying and hiding secret knowledge from them.

There was no secret fire, I never saw the gods themselves. They cannot stand the idea that their world is closer to miracles than mine, that they stand on miracles at the turn of every corner, that they hold miracles in their hands and in each other. These aren't my people. More and more it became clear these were the wealthy, obsessed with the notion of living forever, ready to foul themselves and me if that will buy them one more year.

I never knew his name, and it wouldn't have mattered. He had a knife.

Jacinta got cut stepping between us. I broke his hand with strength I didn't dream to have in me, and before I knew it, that knife was in his neck, his face drenched in sweat, and then…

His chest is open, as I squeeze the blood out of him. I feel a warmth and ecstasy I can't explain. A voice I finally recognize as my own screams:

"The gods have no use for the hearts of cowards."

And I am throwing his heart away, like so much filth. I no longer wear a mask, and though made filthy with gore, I know my skin and flesh are no longer withered. The people bow to me in adoration and fear, all but two. Miguel's mask is off as well, and the fires of ambition burned like a lighthouse. Jacinta is terrified, her cut forearm bandaged with some rag.

She was in his arms, and I believed then that her love for me was lost.

Miguel didn't waste time. Our small gatherings soon became too great and had to be moved to faraway places. I'm told the names and shown their location on maps, but they mean nothing to me. I see myself in the mirrors, beautiful, and feel nothing; whenever I try to hold Jacinta's hand, she shrinks into herself. It lasts a moment but it's always there.

I can't escape my shadow and soon can't stand my own face. I am always wearing the mask, the one I had been buried wearing, and when the time comes for the celebrations, they dress me again in wrappings that imitate the shroud they had found me in.

This is when I broke. They made me mock the rituals of my living days, my faith, my heart. I felt nothing as they made me pluck hearts and anoint these deceivers in human blood.

Meaningless. All pretense was gone, what few people knew better had left long ago in disgust. Whatever monster had killed me, its curse was in full bloom. I was a field of deadly poppies, and these sick animals came to me to die or beg for their lives.

Not content to have me spill their blood, the day came they wished me to spill my own.

"Mind letting them have a taste?" Miguel had asked. "They've been dying to try."

"Let them die then."

He shook his head. "Bad for business. Let's mix it up with something sweet, let them have a taste."

"Madness."

Miguel laughed. "The British were eating mummy flesh. Better a drop of blood, certainly?" He wagged his finger at me. "We'll just run a little test first, why won't we?"

Even in my new state I would not eat or drink. Not until these false rituals started; then I had my fill of blood and would go into a dreamless dark for days at the time. Jacinta, no longer my guardian and fearing to be alone with me, left open the path for Miguel and his men to steal my blood as I slept.

"How do you feel?" Miguel asked Jacinta. "Fine? Well good, but I'm hoping for better than fine." Miguel had brought us together to ambush me, to lay bare his schemes and hold my own heart in his hand and make me look at it. "I've been mixing Anacaona's blood with your food for weeks now."

Jacinta felt sick, as did I. Miguel laughed at what he had done, and made clear he couldn't care less. Jacinta appeared to be fine, so he declared my curse harmless and that he would be selling my blood to his clientele.

It was then my indifference became hate. And if not in love, at least in hate Jacinta returned to me. She was in my arms, weeping at what had been done to us, her head resting on my breast. I took off my mask so I could feel her hair on my cheek; holding her tight, I whispered revenge in her ear.

They must have been thousands. A place had been found for the gathering, a building nestled underground. False icons decorated the walls, and they all stood like the damned, from wall to wall, waiting to receive the blood. It had taken months to arrange it all, and every day until this feast was spent dreaming of destroying them all.

I was made to kill three men and one woman that night. Their fantasies projected upon me, I was made to celebrate this madness nearly naked, and I had refused to wear the mask. In fact, I broke it the day before, to cut my ties with the world that I could never return to.

I was shouted at in more languages than I could imagine to exist, hailed like a living miracle, the answer to the cry of despair born of a thousand throats or more. The sound shook me to my bones and opened a door within me which had been sealed shut.

I was being hunted by the creature that slayed me, but it was from its eyes that I saw myself as I was. My eyes burned with tears surrounded by future people, as reason asserted itself upon my memory. I had not been royalty, a priest, nor some sacrifice: why would I have been given a burial ceremony so lavish? Why hadn't I been cremated?

Something hungry had hunted me and worn my skin. And once wearing me, it had become me and still it must have been outed. I had been sealed and interred, my body wilting, desiccated by the sheer heat and kept away from the eyes of Toci and all her children. I had not been honored: I had been exiled for the good of my people.

And now it was too late. My blood was mixed with the libations and everyone drank deeply of it; I was fed the blood of the sacrifices so they could drink from me. I saw Jacinta, felt her, and knew the time had come.

"Fire!"

The smoke blinded them, and the fear broke through their ecstasy. They vomited blood—my blood—and began to tear at each other, trapped by the mass of bodies, before those at the edges realized they had been trapped underground by all the doors being sealed.

By some miracle Jacinta made her way back to me, though I had told her to leave, and Miguel was there, a gun in his hand. He accused us of treachery and I could have laughed, deafened as we all were by the panic of the bloodied and suffocating crowd. The fire began to eat its way closer to us and the smoke rose higher. I saw it then. The vents, pulling the smoke into them, are too high for them to reach but large enough for someone to squeeze through. I had Jacinta in my arms—drew her nearer still. Miguel shot twice, and the bullets pierced our bodies.

I was never alive.

My skin stretched thin and burst. My wings spread tall and wide, spelling doom. My long thin arms held Jacinta's body closer to mine, covered in black fur. With a clawed foot, I stamped on Miguel and pinned him down.

Those not yet blind and utterly mad cried to me for the mercy of a quick death, if not salvation, and I ignored them. I took to the air and carried my burdens as if they weighed nothing, and crawled through the vents as if I too was smoke. Jacinta, I held gently, safe in my bosom.

Miguel, I dragged, his body bumping against the metal, scraping off skin and clothes.

The sun rose over the shadow strewn hills. No one could hear the screams, but the smoke would alert anyone close enough to see or smell it. Jacinta's eyes would not open, her heartbeat fading, her blood on my lips. I could not give life. Only take, and take, and take. This world of miracles was as deaf to my pleas as gods, old and new, were.

I could not remember who I was before I became myself, but the knowledge of my nature gave me only one answer to this horror. Jacinta's skin stretched in my hands like putty, and I crawled inside her. I will never know if I did it for love or fear of losing myself without a familiar skin to wear. All I know is that the sun's burning gaze found Jacinta slowly rising to her feet, changed, with two hearts beating inside her.

Miguel was dying, but much too slowly. He dragged himself away from me on bruised arms, meowling pitifully. A broken hip rendered him unable to stand. I had no pity left, and when Jacinta spoke, our voices were one.

"We cannot give. But we can take."

And so we turned him around with ease, our strength immense, and we tore the rest of his clothes, and with sharpened fingers that cut like blades, we pried loose his skin without killing him. He was found alive, still screaming himself raw, his muscle and fat exposed to the midday sun.

They would never know how he had lasted so long or what hand undressed him so. We took his tongue along with his skin. If he wishes to write an account of his own, let him use his very blood as ink.

We were not found by the prying eyes of men. We observed, our hearts beating in perfect synchrony, drums in the night, spilling fire.

Beware. We shall rise from the hecatomb, both our beating hearts, again and again, from the fire and the blood, a pillar of smoke. If you beg for forgiveness, do it once and once only, and be sure to mean it and live by it every day of your life.

The gods do not forgive twice, and neither do we.

DEAD KINGS, NO CROWNS

CHRISTOPHER LA VIGNA

"*D-D-D-DJ NesYa in the mix!*"

If you've been hitting the rave scene the last year or two, then there's no chance in hell that you haven't heard that tag from the newest, and already, the biggest DJ in the EDM scene: DJ NesYa. It seemed as though he became a household name—or more accurately, an apartment-hold name since most of us are too broke to buy a home anytime soon—overnight. Nobody knew his real name or where he was from. Shit, no one even knew if he was a he, she, or they, in the sense that some argued DJ NesYa was really a moniker for some kind of sonic collective presenting itself as one insanely prolific DJ.

All people knew was that the dude was dropping the hottest tracks in the game, and he always hit the booth dressed like a mummy whose sarcophagus got dropped into a neon paint factory. He's always wrapped up in these bright green bandages. Beneath the wrappings, he wears some sort of helmet that hides his face behind a black visor. Twin red lights glow behind the glass to represent his unholy gaze washing over the screaming, dancing crowds he observes from his techno throne. He's freakishly tall too, six foot ten at least.

Nobody's been able to get him to give any interviews; apparently he hates podcasts, and no other DJs have spent any time chatting with him in the green room between sets or anything like that. He just dropped his trio of era-defining albums—*TruVoice Volumes I & II*, *Pharaoh Phunk*, and *SethSet(s)*—then started hitting up every club and warehouse that would have him, which was literally all of them because, holy shit, have you heard these records?

He effortlessly combines pretty much every kind of musical influence you could imagine—rock, funk, hip hop, hyperpop, Middle Eastern folk, industrial metal, giallo film scores, the works. It's like he reaches his hands up into the sky with his bandaged palms outstretched, closes them into fists, and pulls down sonic dreamscapes from the ether. He puts it all to a pulsing beat and throws in some dope and downright spooky vocal samples, usually somebody reading from translated Egyptian texts. He's *really* big on the ancient Egypt thing, if that wasn't glaringly obvious. And in these dark days where much of America seems to be engulfed in a twenty-first century Satanic Panic, there are whispers that DJ NesYa might be some kind of occultist trying to spread his pagan magic all around the globe. The rest of us either think that's bullshit or just don't care. Not that it matters much anyway, the dark mystery of it all only seems to make his popularity grow.

———

All that matters is that ya boy Franklin, AKA Frankie Nugs, is at the Boiler Plate event over at that new club in Bushwick to check out DJ NesYa's latest set. I am so fuckin' pumped! I bought some cheap bandages and pins from the pharmacy, so I could come in looking like a mummified raver. I'm buzzing off a couple vodka Redbulls, and I'm waiting for the shrooms I took while I was on the train to finally kick in. This place is pretty damn big, and there's tons of people packed in here. Throngs of people are vibrating on the highest frequencies possible, clad quite scantily in leather shorts, neon t-shirts, and fishnets. Whatever makeup people have chosen to adorn their faces with is already starting to melt off from the extreme humidity brought about by the collective body heat alone.

Drink in hand, I make my way from the bar just off to the side of the entrance and decide to plant myself in the thick of the crowd that's already formed in front of the stage. There's an opening act, a younger up-and-comer by the name of *Dracuul* who is clearly going for some sort of corporate goth vampire theme. She's wearing a black blazer with nothing but a bra underneath, her face caked in white makeup, mouth slathered with fake blood gel from a pop-up Halloween store. The mixes are good, but pretty predictable, lots of samples from old vampire flicks mixed with sped up 80s goth staples. We all give her a polite amount of applause and "Woooos!" as she wraps up and leaves the stage, but it's obvious the crowd is holding back, reserving their true inner animals for the main event.

I take another look around the place as I feel the familiar warmth and tingle of the mushrooms activating, flowing up my spine, nuzzling around the base of my neck. They really went all out decorating the place. There's all these big sarcophagi leaned up against the walls, and above them are the graffiti-like murals full of hieroglyphs. It's like they got Keith Haring or Jean-Michel Basquiat to decorate the interior of King Tut's tomb, space and time incongruities be damned. There are cameras all over the place too; Boiler Plate's big on live-streaming their raves. I can even spot a few people sporting Go-Pro rigs on their heads, likely some volunteers who are going to provide the frenetic crowd-POV shots. Hundreds of thousands of people will be watching tonight. No doubt about it, DJ NesYa is going to dominate, and the big world takeover starts tonight.

It dawns on me that everything I see looks like it's being shot through a wide-angle lens. Every sound that rushes into my ears has a stuttering echo. The very edges of my peripheral vision seem to be distorting, and now I know for certain that I am peaking on the shrooms, and it is a glorious thing, made all the better when the house lights dim again, and the crowd erupts in a mighty roar of excitement as the king of the night enters stage right.

He's changed up his look for tonight too. His bandages have a kind of inverted rainbow coloring to them—I don't know how else to describe it—like a rainbow blazing through a jet-black night sky. These two massive guys dressed up like Set, the Egyptian God of Chaos, trail behind him with bullet belts crisscrossed over their bare chests. They must be on stilts or something, the way they tower over him. As DJ NesYa marches up to the steps, takes his place behind the booth, and slips on his headphones, his head slowly pans across the room, studying all of us with cold indifference. The giant Set guards take their places on opposite sides of the booth, arms folded.

With the quick press of a few buttons, the music starts up, a looping synth bass riff gradually building in speed. A spotlight shines down on the mummified DJ and the glittering glow of his high-fashion bandages. The crowd erupts in applause once again, the mere addition of an extra light being enough to rile 'em up. But the light tilts up and widens out, revealing a massive disco ball pyramid behind him. The light hits the glass surface and bounces refractions of rainbow light waves into our collectively wide-opened eyes. I'm forced to avert my gaze to keep from being blinded.

The song is still building, teasing us with a beat drop that will crash down on our heads like a rockslide. Everybody's dancing, but mostly just two-stepping it, grooving a little with the synths, but waiting until the big drop comes to really go insane. My eyes are locked on DJ NesYa, and all I can think about at this moment is how eerily still he is. For a split second, I swear those glowing ruby eyes of his are staring at me, directly boring into my soul. My mind goes to war with itself; one half is convinced that he's trying to tell me something, trying to communicate on a telepathic level, while the other half is screaming that this is just the shrooms kicking in, and I need to relax already.

I see DJ NesYa break his stillness, one arm reaching out, pulling a slider down, lowering the bass loop. He then introduces a new layer, some ethereal chords that sound like they come from the string section of an invisible orchestra. Everything slows down now; with one little switch up, he's turned the air into amber, and we're all nothing more than mosquitoes frozen within it. He moves his other hand to hit a glowing red button to the center left of the console. Without warning, a strange voice blares out through the massive speakers, a voice that sounds like a battle cry from the ancient dead filtered through digital vocal cords:

"Hear me now, all servants of Set
All mortals who yearn for the riches and glories of
the afterlife

You are beset on all sides by the tyrannies of
false kings
These are not your pharaohs, your great kings
They are little more than greedy merchants bleeding
you dry
Cast them off and ascend to the throne of Set!
Take your place at the right hand of the dark God
of Chaos!"

The bass loop kicks up again, rising up until it's glid-
ing just beneath the strings and vocals. The crowd is
vibrating, dancing, vibing out, but I'm standing there
as still as DJ NesYa, absorbing his words…

"Hear the voice of the mighty Nesyamun
High priest of Egypt
Listen to this hymn, a song of revolution against
the veil
Between mortality and eternity
All the world shall be a pyramid
Dead Kings, No Crowns
DEAD KINGS, NO CROWNS!"

Everybody starts chanting along with this: DEAD
KINGS, NO CROWNS, building up towards a massive
crescendo. Even though I'm shouting along to it, a big
part of me is starting to fear that something downright
demonic is going down. And then, at long last, the beat
drops, and all hell breaks loose.

A bass kick heavy enough to shake the building's foundation hits, and the pulsing beat sends the chanting crowd into a frenzy. A cloud of gritty brown-red mist that reeks like copper shoots out from the stage, spreading everywhere, plunging us all into a man-made sandstorm. The strobing lights from the stage and the disco pyramid are the only thing keeping it all from going pitch black, and in the chaos I can see bodies being lifted into the air, struggling in vain against the forces picking them up and toying with them like rag dolls. They scream as the sands whip at their flesh, pour down their throats, then whip right back out, sucking their fluids, their lifeforce, their very souls out of them.

I rush over to one side of the room, doing my best to hug the wall and stay clear of the stampede of frightened people trying to run like hell away from this. I'm hyperventilating, and I realize the bandages on my face are covering my nose and mouth, the only thing keeping the sands from snaking into me and bleeding me dry. I take countless elbows to the back, get my feet stomped on until I'm sure I have more than a few broken bones in each of them, but I stay upright.

The surviving people have made their way to the front door and the emergency exits, but all of the doors are locked. I can hear panicked voices shouting commands over each other as they try to figure out how to bust the doors open. I remember that I saw some windows above the stalls in the men's room on the opposite side of the place. That might be my only shot out of here. I bolt towards the bathrooms, doing my best not to step on anybody. I glance over to the stage, and DJ NesYa is still there, but his creepy stillness is gone. Now he's dancing to his own insane music, his Set-dressed guards pumping their fists to the beat in unison. For them, the ritualistic sacrifice party is still raging on.

I'm still moving towards the restrooms when I feel something grip my ankle. I look down, and I see it's one of the desiccated raver corpses, but somehow it's moving, its sunken eyes glaring at me, its wide opened mouth moaning with hunger.

I scream, knowing full well that no one can hear me over the indoor sandstorm and the countless other cries. I try to brush this monster off, but its bony fingers dig into my ankle, and I fall trying to sprint away from it.

The dried zombie crawls on top of me, its hands reaching for my face, trying to peel the bandages off. It wants me to breathe in the dust. It wants me to join the rest of them. I find the strength to grab it by its shoulders and throw it off of me. I can hear most of its bones cracking as it lands on the floor. I'm scrambling back on my feet, blitzing over to the bathrooms. I can see what has to be at least a hundred or so of these mummified things getting up, shuffling around, attacking what few humans were still here.

As I get closer, I pass one of the bars that just moments ago was completely surrounded by care-free people knocking back drinks and socializing. Now it was completely abandoned, the bartender now one of the zombie husks, idling around liquor bottles that all look to be filled with blood.

None of this makes any sense, but I don't have time to figure out a mystery. If I don't get out of here, I'm going to be torn to shreds. I remind myself of this as I finally reach the men's room, kicking the door down and rushing towards the stalls.

In my peripheral, I see the bathroom mirror has been smashed, and a message has been scrawled in blood over the cracked surface: NESYAMUN LIVES!

I rush to the last stall on the left and open the door, coming face to face with another sentient corpse. This one is trying to drape itself in toilet paper, a vain attempt to make itself look like a proper mummy. Enraged by my interruption, it drops the roll of toilet paper and lunges at me. Even though its arms look like twigs with dead skin stretched over them, its grip around my throat is tight. I can feel the pressure threatening to crush my larynx as it lifts me up in the air.

I swing my leg back and kick it in the chest, sending the brittle remains of its rib cage shattering out of its back. It collapses to the floor in a heap, moaning angrily at me as I stand on the toilet and boost myself up onto the window ledge.

Of course, the window's locked, but I take advantage of my pre-bandaged fists and punch a few holes into the frosted glass. I push myself over the windowsill and take a solid drop onto the hard plastic lid of the dumpster below, rolling off of it and flopping onto the pavement.

I limp around the back of the building up to the street. When I get to the front of the warehouse, I see that somebody's parked DJ NesYa's tour bus right outside the entrance, blocking the doors. There are no bounc-ers in sight. The people trapped inside have no way of escaping, but the force they're exerting on the door is enough that I can see the bus shaking.

I start to walk out onto the street, realizing I dropped my phone inside, trying to figure out who I can call for help, when I hear the heavy metallic groan of the bus being turned on its side. The *BOOM* of its crashing shakes me once more, and I fall to my knees. I look back and see the bus being pushed forward as the warped metal doors of the warehouse slowly open. Those bloody dust clouds waft out into the open air, springing like tornadoes, rushing out into the streets, eager to spread their plague.

I hear the collective moans of the mummified ravers and can see dozens of them shambling on top of the bus, crawling around the sides. All I can do is run as best I can, especially when I hear DJ NesYa's tech-enabled voice calling, echoing out into the cold night "DEAD KINGS, NO CROWNS. Let the world become a tomb!"

The sands are swirling everywhere now, expanding down the streets. I just keep running until I make it to the Kosciuszko Bridge, when I feel like I've finally outrun the sandstorm of the damned. I hike my way up the stairs, ready to hoof it over to Queens. But when I take a moment to breathe, I look out at the skyline, and I can see red-brown storm clouds hovering over the boroughs. I can hear screams and groans rising up like an unholy chorus. DJ NesYa, Nesyamun—whatever he chose to call himself—his curse was spreading everywhere. There is nowhere to run. Just as he said, the world is becoming one giant pyramid, a tomb filled with the mummified remains of all humankind. We'll all be pharaohs in this new world—dead kings, no crowns.

I close my eyes, pull the bandages down, and breathe in the future that Nesyamun has given us.

#RICH-TOK

B.F. VEGA

The envelope had a strange scent, warm and earthy with a hint of licorice. There was no stamp, and no return address.

"What's this?" Justin asked as Mat, his dad's secretary, handed him the envelope. Mat merely shrugged his ignorance as he left the room.

Justin turned the envelope over a few times. Maybe there was something he wasn't seeing? But it simply had Justin's full name, Justinian Andrew Bennet-Hallingsworth III, spelled out in precise calligraphy.

Justin shrugged his own shoulders and ripped the side of the envelope open. A single piece of cardstock was inside.

The card was an invitation. It had a picture of a supine Egyptian mummy flanked by two goddesses with wings. Above the picture it said:

Thursday the 12th of March
in the year of our lord 20--
830 Reed Field Way
A mummy to be unwrapped for scientific
and personal curiosity
Half-past the midnight hour.
Dress in appropriate Victorian regalia.
No phones. The event will be live-streamed
anonymously #Rich-Tok

Justin smiled at the odd little paper. This had to be Aster. She was the only one of his friends kooky enough for this sort of thing. He checked his phone to see if she had posted something about it yet, but she hadn't. That was just like her, keeping things mysterious until the last minute. Speaking of the last minute, it was already three in the afternoon of the eleventh and he needed to come up with Victorian eveningwear.

"Mat," he yelled out without bothering to get up from his chair. "Mat, I need you to do something for me."

———

A little past midnight Justin stopped the Porsche his dad had given him for his twentieth birthday. The GPS said that he should turn in one hundred feet, but there didn't seem to be a street there. He crawled down the road and as the GPS said "turn right now," he saw a dark gap between the two buildings to his right, barely larger than his car. He stopped and backed up so he could make the turn.

Even in the little sports car, the alley Justin found himself in was tight. It ran for two blocks before giving out onto a wide cul-de-sac with four large homes. He didn't have to double-check to know he was in the right place. He recognized Tim's BMW, Janet's Mercedes, and Aster's Volvo sitting in front of a large late-Georgian home. He parked and began the process of pulling himself out of the car without tearing the rather tight Victorian morning suit that Mat had come up with at the last minute. He chucked his phone into the in-car safe and pulled the top hat out. He placed the hat on his head of mahogany curls.

As he walked up to the door he wondered why he had never seen this street before. All the homes were immaculate. He pushed the doorbell and waited a moment. He heard footsteps approaching and then the door was opened by a tall lithe man dressed in an all-black silk suit. The man had sun-darkened skin and eyes as black as his father's Bugatti.

"Good evening, sir. Are you Mr. Bennet-Hallingsworth?"

"I am the Junior Bennet-Hallingsworth," Justin answered. He hated being a third. Especially as his grandfather and father were both still alive. Sometimes it meant that he was mistaken as one of them so he had become very careful how he answered that question.

"Ah, very good. Mr. Justin, I assume then?" the man said.

Justin nodded.

"If you will follow me, sir." The man waved Justin in and closed the door behind him. Inside, the floor was milky alabaster. Justin had never seen an alabaster floor before and it took his breath away for a moment. The hallway was lit with sconces that held Edison bulbs. This created pools of light along the long hall. The wall itself seemed to be papered with what looked like hand-painted nineteenth-century Chinese wallpaper. The wallpaper showed beautiful electric blue lotuses and tall reeds along the baseboards and ducks flying along the top.

Justin was accustomed to wealth, but this was astounding.

The man who had answered the door led Justin to a door at the other end of the hall. He knocked on it and a small panel slid open. Eyes like liquid gold, rimmed in heavy black eyeliner, looked out at them.

"Mr. Justin," the man said.

The panel slid shut and the heavy oak door opened. A woman stood in front of Justin. She was clad in a long white gown that hugged every curve intimately. Her long black hair was as straight as a freeway in the desert and of course, those liquid gold eyes were paired with a mouth the color of fine port. Justin instinctively took off his top hat and held it in front of himself to add some extra protection to the tight pants.

The woman smiled at his obvious admiration and beckoned him forward. As he passed the heavy oak door, she pulled it closed behind her and for a moment they were plunged into blackness.

"Apologies," she purred in his ear. He could feel her warmth behind him, and he again smelled the scent from the letter. Deep and warm. He heard a click and lights came on again in the sconces. The lights led down a set of broad curving stairs.

The woman handed him an LED taper candle and indicated that he should follow her.

He did so, only tripping once when he was paying too much attention to her plump backside and not enough attention to the granite stairs.

At the bottom of the stairs, she indicated a doorway to his left.

"Thank you," he said and reminded himself to get Aster to introduce them later. He opened the door and found that he was looking down into an old Victorian operating theater. There were four sections of audience seating, each separated by glass. The bottom of the seating section was also glassed off. Justin walked down the four rows of seats and chose a seat at the bottom. The mummy was already laying on the surgical table. Beside it was a small surgical tray with scissors, some scalpels, and an intricate dagger that looked to be made out of some sort of mineral, malachite maybe. The hilt was alternating bands of gold and lapis lazuli.

Justin was perplexed. The mummy didn't look dark enough. He had seen mummies at the Cairo Museum when his family had gone, but this one looked brand new. The wrappings were snow-white. How could it have survived in such great condition?

Justin looked up and was surprised to see Aster sitting in the viewing section opposite him. Tim was in the section to his right, and Janet was in the section to his left.

He looked at Aster and tried to speak. The glass was apparently soundproof as she cupped her hand to her ear, but shook her head to indicate that she couldn't hear him.

She seemed to be an invitee and that worried Justin a little. If Aster hadn't organized this, who had and why?

A blinking light above him caught his attention and he saw that there were cameras throughout the theater. One was pointed straight at him. He remembered that the invite had said whatever was about to happen would be live-streamed, so he put his top hat back on in a jaunty fashion and winked at it.

A door to the surgery theater opened below, and a man walked into the circular room. He was dressed in a long white operating gown and had a round white cap on his head. His face was covered in a large white mask that left only his eyes visible.

The man looked up at one of the cameras and waved. He then picked up a pair of scissors and, without acknowledging the four friends in their separate viewing sections, he snipped into the first set of bandages.

Justin knew something was wrong as soon as the "surgeon" had pulled aside the first set of bandages. The set underneath was a dark rusted color. He had seen dried blood before. He had helped his father and Mat scrub the tiles after his stepmother's "accident." He had been sick afterward. The dried blood on the bandages triggered something inside of him and he felt the bile rising in his throat like it had that horrible night. He knew his father hadn't meant to kill her. His father was usually a reasonable man. It was the alcohol and the drugs that made him pick up the golf club and beat her until her blood and brains were permanently stained into the carpet of their family room.

He remembered his stepsister's sorrow when he told her that her mom had left and that he had no idea where she was. He felt the pain in his stomach from when his stepsister had cried and begged him to go to the police with her, to help her find the woman he knew to be dead.

As Justin sat above the operating theater, he envisioned the bloodied rug where the mummy currently lay. His stomach dropped. Panic surged through him. He had to get away. He bolted up from his seat and ran up toward the door. He grabbed the handle only to discover that it was locked.

"Let me out!" he yelled and was rewarded with another panel opening and the golden eyes staring into his.

"Not until the performance is over. It's a safety precaution, you understand," the woman said in her low throaty growl of a voice. "Besides, you don't want to embarrass yourself on Rich-Tok, do you?"

Justin remembered the cameras. He turned to see that all of them were pointed at him now. He wondered if they were really live-streaming.

"We have over 50,000 viewers tonight," the golden-eyed one said. "Some of your own followers have already started commenting."

Justin looked up at the cameras as she spoke, then decided it was best not to make a scene on the off chance she was telling the truth. The last thing he needed was for the world at large to wonder why dried blood made him panic. He slowly walked back to his seat. He saw that the surgeon was looking straight at him. He looked up and his three friends were also slowly walking back to their seats. He realized that they were all locked in and from the looks of it, the other three had no idea what was actually going on either.

He locked eyes with the surgeon. There was something familiar about him. Without breaking eye contact, Justin sat down and then gestured to the surgeon to continue.

A spark of something that could have been humor or surprise flashed through the surgeon's eyes at Justin's gesture. But he straightened his shoulders and then bowed as if responding to a command from the king.

The surgeon returned to the table. Once again taking the shears, he cut another long slit from the mummy's groin to its neck. The dried blood was more visible at this layer. It fanned out across the mummy's chest in varying shades of red down to a black, inky spot above the mummy's right hip. The surgeon turned toward a camera. He pressed down on the bandages near the wound. Under his hand, blood welled up, running through his fingers and down the side of the mummy.

Justin's eyes widened. What kind of a mummy bleeds? Was it… actually still alive?

The surgeon held his blood-soaked hand up in front of his face.

Justin's breath caught in his throat, certain that the man would lick his hand clean. The surgeon locked eyes with him then, grinning slightly beneath the surgical mask. He then lowered his bloodied hand and wiped it with a nearby towel. Justin's body went limp with relief.

He looked across to his friends. Aster was up against the glass partition with tears streaming down her face. Tim was rocking back and forth in his seat with his hands over his ears and his eyes closed tightly. With alarm, Justin realized he couldn't see Janet. He rushed down to the glass partition hopeful that she was just hidden from his view.

Instead he found that the surgeon had moved and was directly in front of Justin's viewing window. The surgeon looked at him with a smile and gestured Justin back toward his seat.

Unsure what else to do, Justin sat down. The surgeon waited until Justin nodded, then he went back to the mummy and picked up the shears again. With every snip of the shears, Justin's sense of unease spread until every muscle was imbued with a feeling of aching sickness.

There were two more layers of increasingly fresh blood and bandages. Each layer was dealt with like the first until only a thin sodden layer of crimson bandages concealed the body from Justin's horrified eyes.

The surgeon stopped once more, scissors raised to Justin asking for permission to cut into the final layer. Justin hesitated, loathe to be sucked into this sick ritual any further. He wondered what would happen if he just didn't move.

The surgeon stared unblinking up at him. Finally, after a few breathless seconds, the surgeon moved the shears and pointed to Tim's now empty seat. Justin felt his heart plummet. He quickly looked up at Aster. She was still there, now curled up in the fetal position, sobbing.

Justin looked back down at the surgeon who stood patiently waiting for Justin's permission. When he caught Justin's eye, he started to move the shears toward Aster's seat. Justin sat down quickly, breathing heavily to keep the hysterics at bay. He shockingly raised his hand, granting permission to finish the task.

When the surgeon cut into the final layer of linen to expose milky white un-desiccated flesh, Justin could no longer deny what was in front of him.

Whatever was going on here, that was no ancient mummy.

The face of the mummy was obscured, but he knew it was female from the exposed torso. The surgeon then turned toward the surgical tray and picked up the ornate dagger. Facing the mummy, the surgeon held the dagger high and said something Justin couldn't hear due to the soundproofing of the glass.

The door of the surgery opened again and the woman with the golden eyes entered, followed by the man who had greeted him at the door.

The surgeon plunged the dagger into the exposed torso and the mummy sat up with a scream that penetrated even the soundproofing.

Justin was on his feet in a flash. He didn't know how the corpse on the table could be alive, especially with a dagger through its heart, but he instinctively knew that he had to help them.

He ran back up the stairs and threw his whole body at the door. It immediately gave under his weight. It took him a moment to register that the door must have been already opened a bit for that to happen.

On the small landing, he saw a door labeled "surgery." He opened it and almost leaped down the short staircase leading down to the operating theater. He had been hearing the screams of the mummy ever since it had first shrieked and now the screams were becoming louder, more persistent.

Justin burst into the theater and stopped. The woman in the white dress and the man in the suit were leaning over the mummy. They steadied themselves with their hands on the surgery table as their mouths got closer to the body. They looked up and growled at him as he entered. He watched as the woman's sleek black hair became fur and a long feline tail dipped out of the back of her gown.

The man, meanwhile, grew taller. His face stretched and elongated as fur began to cover his exposed flesh. His ears moved to the top of his head and his eyes moved closer together, until his face was more jackal-like than human.

Losing interest in Justin, the lion woman opened her jaw and tore a chunk from the exposed torso of the screaming mummy.

The jackal man dug his maw mid-snout into the opening the lion woman created and snapped at the mummy's intestines. He pulled a long section out and ate it like noodles, slurping it up and then going back for more.

Justin turned to try and retreat. The surgeon blocked his way.

"I'm surprised it was you," the surgeon said in Mat's voice. "I thought you would try to run away instead of helping her." He pulled a scalpel from his pocket and placed it against Justin's Adam's apple.

"Mat… But why? What is this?" Justin asked.

"Rich-Tok. And Sekhmet and Anubis need to feed." With that, Mat pushed Justin toward a door opposite the one he had used to enter the operating theater. Once on the other side of the door, he found himself in the room where all the cameras were streaming to. Alongside the streaming carnage was a sick scroll of people commenting with glee about the mummy's fate.

@SickKitt: Hell Yeah! #EatTheRich!!

@BluHypo: Hope those are some rich and tasty noodles, Anubis!

@SkyMommy: Yes! Sekmet's pulling out the heart, it's my favorite part!

@BabiDaddi: Hope she doesn't get heart burn!

Justin turned away from the screen and vomited on the floor at Mat's feet.

Mat calmly stepped aside from the pooling vomit before continuing. "The cameras are of course live streaming to a dark website called Rich-Tok. We follow #Rich-Tok kids online, selecting the most annoying rich kids and then mummifying them alive, which preserves their bodies well enough until Sekhmet and Anubis get hungry."

Justin looked at the screens. He saw all three of his friends being stripped and tied down to embalming tables. He watched as someone he couldn't identify picked up a thin hooked instrument and approached Tim.

Tim screamed as the brain extractor broke through his nasal passage and started scrambling his frontal cortex.

He wanted to turn away, or close his eyes, anything to make the horrific scenes stop but he couldn't take his eyes off of his friends, one by one having their brains removed while they screamed and cried. When the bandaging started, he turned to Mat. But where Mat had been was now a creature with the snout of a crocodile and the mane of a lion.

"What? What are you?" Justin managed to gasp out.

"I am Ammit, the devourer of the hearts of sinners. And I am very hungry."

ONE HUNDRED DEAD CATS

KRISTIN DEARBORN

"There used to be so many mummies people burned them to keep warm," Dan said.

"Wow." Valeria let go of the crate they'd guided across the warehouse floor and immediately pulled out her phone. The screen lit her face in the dim room.

"They used to eat them, make paint out of them, and ones like these were used as fertilizer for crops."

Valeria raised her gaze from her screen.

"Ate them?"

Dan inhaled, ready to give an explanation.

"Never mind, I don't want to know."

"It's history."

"It's morbid and gross. And it's gross that we're moving a hundred dead cats."

"They're headed to the museum tomorrow."

"Not soon enough, if you ask me. It's already been dropped, and they'd better not blame us."

"I took pictures when it got here. I don't think it's too bad."

Dan lowered the pallet jack and deposited the large wooden box on the warehouse floor. Indeed, one corner was crumpled and damaged. He hated to see anything come in with damage. Someone from the museum would be here at eight tomorrow morning, so they staged the box in front of the loading bay door, ready to go.

"Can I go?" Valeria had her phone out again.

"You don't think it's cool that we're moving a piece of history?"

"We're moving dead cats. I like cats. I have two. What a weird week it's been. When are the Smiths coming for the acid? I don't like having that here, either."

"Oh," Dan said. "It's actually not acid, not exactly. It's a highly corrosive combination of—"

"Dan, go home. Go home and get away from the dead cats. I hope Timothy and Felix aren't seeing this. It's nasty."

The crate of mummies was emblazoned with a bright red "fragile" sign, and a "this side up." They'd treated it with the utmost respect, mostly because Dan was a little obsessed with all things ancient Egypt. Valeria spent her time bitching about moving "dead cats."

Timothy was, indeed, watching all this. And listening. He and Felix lived in the warehouse, originally as pest control, a job Felix took to with gusto. Timothy… Timothy was more in the public relations field, schmoozing with guests and boosting morale in the office. He'd been asleep this morning (big surprise) when the crate came in, and with it, a smell unlike anything he'd ever encountered. Timothy was a neutered tomcat, a big boy, white with tabby spots. He carried his bulk gracefully, and as the warehouse lights switched off, he sauntered to the crate. Dan said it was full of dead cats. The idea made him jumpy. During lunch, where Timothy sat at Dan's feet willing him to drop some meat from his sandwich (he did), Dan told him all about how the Egyptians worshiped cats and made them into mummies so the cats would continue on into the afterlife with their owners.

It sounded like hogwash to Timothy. It didn't take human intervention to get a cat to the afterlife, to the Heaviside Layer. Sounded even worse when Dan told him that people would *kill* the cats to mummify them for their own selfish reasons. A crate holding a hundred of his murdered brethren, from… how long ago? Dan hadn't said, but they were old.

"I like talking to you, Tim," Dan said, slipping him a piece of turkey. "You actually give a shit about my stories."

Usually Timothy just wanted the turkey, but today he was truly interested. He gave an encouraging "miaw" hoping Dan would go on. But lunch was over, and everyone went back to work. Timothy positioned himself to watch Dan and Valeria at the end of the day, but Valeria didn't want to hear about the dead cats.

With the warehouse closed down for the night, Timothy approached the crate. He moved slowly, with twin motivations of respect and fear. The smells baffled him. An underlying smell of cat, yes, but also pine—and Timothy could discern between the wood making up the crate itself and the contents within. Faint pine, ancient pine. Maybe beeswax. And pistachio, which made Timothy think of Valeria sharing her ice cream with him on a summer afternoon. He had no doubt this was what Dan said it was, a box of dead cats.

He sat, pondering the box. Troubled by the humans' idea that this "mummification" process was the cats' ticket to the afterlife. A cat was supposed to die with dignity, alone, on his or her own terms. Timothy knew of cats taken away, surrounded by people, killed and burned. He didn't know if that impeded the journey to the Heaviside Layer, but he certainly didn't want to find out. Dan said the organs were removed, and the cats (and people, and crocodiles, and any other thing these people got their hands on) were wrapped in resin and linen to preserve them. Preservation was the most important thing.

However, preservation was impossible, because everything went back to the earth eventually. Humans fancied themselves masters of keeping things longer than they ought to. Took great pride in it.

Timothy jumped on top of the crate. The moment his paws touched the wood, a jolt of something rocked him. *Free them. Get them out. Let them back to Earth so they can ascend.* He hopped back to the concrete floor, but the pads of his paws still tingled. A hundred voices in his head, crying for liberation and a chance. He studied the crate. Built for travel, sturdy. Hard for a cat to penetrate. One dented corner seemed to be the only point where he could even slide a paw in. He lowered his pink nose to the black hole in the corner, and sniffed. Cats. He needed to help them.

For being a large cat, poor Timothy was often mocked for his delicate white paws. He didn't see why it was a big deal, as his paws did what he needed them to do. They weren't ugly polydactyl behemoths like Felix's lynx-like cartoon feet. He reached in, tentative, careful and… ouch! Something sharp. He yanked his paw back, but snagged it on a splinter and had to push forward into the crate to get himself free. He could feel his pad bleeding, and when he drew it back, he paused halfway to his mouth. He shook his foot, spattering blood into the crate. He didn't want to clean it with his tongue.

Something shifted inside the crate. Magic is not unfamiliar to cats, evolution can't be credited for all of their luck. The magic swirling in the crate was green (don't ask Timothy how he knew that, as it was still confined in the crate) and he wasn't sure it was good. He scuttled back, leaving bloody paw prints behind him.

The crate shook. The fresh wood holding it together groaned in protest as something inside moved. Timothy's ears flattened on his skull, and his fur fluffed, tail growing large. He'd been in this warehouse a long time, and not much got to him like this. He hissed. There were workers who'd been here half a decade and never heard him hiss. A growl rumbled low in his throat.

Had he made a mistake? *No*, he thought. Wouldn't he be upset if foolish humans kept him from the Heaviside Layer for centuries?

A paw flashed out from the broken corner of the crate. But not a normal, healthy paw, rather one swaddled in ancient linen. Timothy wanted to help, but the memory of that sharp pain kept him back. He still couldn't bring himself to clean his wound.

Another paw, similarly shrouded, appeared. Then another. And another. What had Dan said? A hundred cat mummies. Where was Felix?

The crate's wood gave under the pressure of all those paws, and the first of the cats slunk out. Its motions were constricted by the layers of wrapping all around it, and where its eyes should have been glowed green. Free, it shook itself, but its wrappings stayed in place. The vibrant green eyes fixated on Timothy. He puffed again and hissed. The other cat arched its back as well, only now two of its companions flanked it, with more fighting their way free as the hole widened.

The cats stumbled out of the crate and its iridescent light. A few of them were concerned with Timothy, but most of them were trying to get their bearings. They looked around, confused and stumbling. They flowed out like a river, one hundred dead cats.

The hell are you doing? Felix appeared from nowhere on the shelving above him. He loomed large, fluffy and intimidating. He had Maine Coon in him. His words left Timothy feeling like a chastised child.

They needed help, Timothy explained. *All those souls.*

Felix grunted. While Timothy came from a humane society and had the dimmest memories of being a cat in a house, Felix came from the streets. "Semi-feral" with a notch in his ear, no one shared lunch with Felix. The big tom made a point to take as little from the humans as he could. He claimed to only stick around because the rats and mice were so plentiful here.

Timothy scurried up to the platform where Felix perched, struggling a bit to get up because of his bulk. They looked down at the confused travelers, ambling around the warehouse floor. The first of the cat mummies through the crate raised his head to Timothy and Felix and fixed those glowing green not-quite-eyes on them. It hissed, and Timothy hissed back.

Save your breath, Felix said. *And try and bring your fluff down. Your human friend never told you how to put these souls to rest? He only told you how to wake them?*

No! I didn't mean to do it! Timothy explained about his paw and the blood. *I was being nosy. And Dan thinks the ancient ones felt they did the cats a favor by wrapping them up and mummifying them.*

I don't see how we can set all of them free, though, Felix said. *There are so many. And I don't even know if that would do it.*

Maybe destroying them would do the trick, Timothy thought. In which case, Dan's horrified stories of mummies being destroyed for fertilizer or paint didn't seem so bad if it released their spirits safely.

Try that one, Felix gestured with his head at one of the cat mummies who strayed from the flock.

Me? Timothy gaped at him.

You started this, boy. You're the one who wouldn't let sleeping cats lie.

Timothy knew Felix had a better shot at getting down there and back. Timothy'd struggled to climb up here. He tried to think of the last time he hunted a mouse. Last week one ran into him, and he'd pounced, but before that… Timothy saw his job here as moral support. A mascot. Sitting on Valeria's lap while she worked at the computer. Greeting visitors with a friendly leg rub. Felix clearly had pest control covered.

As stealthily as he could muster, Timothy dropped from the shelf. Behind him, Felix yowled. All the green eyes fixed on the elder cat. Timothy's quarry ambled off on its own, on her own. He sensed she was female from the way she moved, even though the ancient linens bound her awkwardly. He scurried for her, favoring his injured paw, and tackled her to the floor. He bit at the ancient linen binding her, the pine and pistachio scent fully flooding his nose. He sneezed. Tore at the cloth that had bound her for thousands of years. She tried to fight, but the strips of linen covered her claws and teeth. She moaned. After so many years the linen came away easily under his claws, and he could feel it getting caught in them. The taste filled his mouth, dry and unpleasant. He didn't know the word for desert, had no concept of what a desert was, but it was the taste filling his mouth. It reminded him of the dust in his litter box, the gritty clay under his paws. He coughed and kept pulling.

Whoever did this to her painted a false face over hers. Exaggerated eyes, a wide mouth. He destroyed the painted stripes on her wrappings. One piece held, and he pulled, a long satisfying strip coming free. He caught a glimpse of dried skin underneath; she made a muffled gasping sound, and the green glow left her eyes and rose like a snake, dissipating before reaching the warehouse ceiling.

To the Heaviside Layer? He didn't know, but the ancient cat lay still. At peace? Timothy hoped so as he realized Felix's attention-getting only worked for so long. The others felt the demise of their companion and wheeled on him. He puffed again. Hissed. He couldn't help himself. He heard ninety-nine hisses around him and galloped to the closest shelving unit. Timothy bounded up a staircase of crates, up to the first level of shelves, and made the harder jump up to the second level. Felix waited there to greet him.

I think it worked, he panted.

There's too many of them. I don't know how we get them all.

The mummies gathered around their fallen comrade. But more still squeezed out of the opening on the crate. One's wrappings caught on the jagged wood and pulled. The creature took three steps before the illuminated eyes winked out.

They're fragile and clumsy, Timothy said.

But there are too many of them, and they're angry. What happens when Dan comes in tomorrow? Or Valeria?

Timothy hadn't thought of that. It embarrassed him that Felix was the one to bring it up; Felix who claimed not to like the humans.

Do you think I helped her?

The bigger cat looked down his nose at Timothy. *At this point, it doesn't matter. They have to be stopped. They can't get out of the warehouse.*

Timothy watched the swirling insanity below. A few of the cats were much larger. Those ones could reach up onto some of the boxes, despite their wrappings and rigor mortis movements. Some of the cats were only kittens. So small. Those tended to stay closer to the crate and bumble around in circles.

We need to move, Timothy, Felix said. *Move or fight.*

You can fight, Timothy said. Felix's ears went back, his eyes narrowed. *Can't you?*

I came here because I don't want to fight. I'm tired of it.

Timothy straightened. *There. That barrel. Valeria says it's acid, Dan says it's not, but whatever it is, they say it'll melt anything it touches.* The barrel sat on a tall shelf, bright yellow with red warning labels.

Including us. We can burn them. That space heater in the office. Send the whole place up in flames and run for it.

No! Timothy couldn't imagine this, the only home he'd ever known, disappearing.

I still think we should run. Forget it ever happened and find someplace new. You'd get scooped up into a home in a heartbeat. It didn't feel kind when Felix said that.

One of the larger cats hauled itself onto the platform directly below them. The linens rustled and the distinct smell wafted up to them.

Felix growled. *You don't have time to figure out how to open a barrel.*

The big cat put two shrouded, exploratory paws up on their level. The lime-colored eyes-not-eyes clocked Timothy and Felix, and the antagonist hissed. His throat and mouth being a thousand years old, it came out like a hollow rattle. Timothy shuddered. Felix arched his back and responded with a proper hiss, launching himself at the other cat. He grappled onto his enemy's face, using his back feet to tear at the other's throat. The other cat was so much bigger, but Felix was *Felix*, worldly and savage. Felix destroyed rats like a machine. He was brutal and systematic, his approach to this stranger was no different. The two lost their footing and slipped, dropping to the shelf below, bringing them closer to the waiting horde. Felix got a strand of the linen wrapping in his mouth and gave a mighty tug. Timothy held his breath; it didn't seem to work the way it had with the others; the big cat kept fighting.

Then the eyes went blank, and the large body drooped. Felix lay still a moment, long enough for a wave of fear to submerge Timothy, but then the tomcat rose, shrugged off the body of the ancient foe, and bounced up onto the shelving where Timothy waited. Felix shook himself and went to work smoothing his long fur.

The acid, Timothy said. *I can knock the barrel over.*

Felix was deadly serious. *If it doesn't work I'm going to burn it all down with the space heater. These things are… I've never seen anything like it.*

Timothy studied the barrel, with its bright warning labels, the way it perched on the edge of its pallet. If he hit it right, his weight would tip it over. That he was sure of. But it was designed for travel, to keep the noxious material safe within. Timothy scurried closer to it, skimming over the boxes and other things prepped for travel. The barrel was so much larger than himself. Was Felix's plan the better way to go? Easier, sure, but everything here would be lost, instead of the few items sitting on the warehouse floor. Felix and Timothy might be lost as well… no guarantee they'd get out if the whole place went up in flames.

Down below, the mummies milled and churned over each other. Strange almost-yowls and meows, ancient and rusty, chilled Timothy. He studied the acid barrel. If he went up another level and hit it at an angle… but would it break when it landed?

He'd only have one shot, and if it didn't work, then Felix would send them all into an inferno. Meanwhile, the other cat made his way to the office.

Timothy climbed. It wasn't his strong suit. He huffed as he made his way up to the next level, the air warming as he climbed closer to the ceiling. At times he had to scrabble, back paws not connecting, each time fearing he'd lose his footing and drop to the floor below. Even if he could land on his feet, would he have time to get away before that awful, rustling mass overcame him?

Felix never believed in him and thought he was just a soft house cat. He was more than that. No cat was "just" a house cat. Each of them brought more to life than just being a plush toy for the humans. They weren't dogs, for heaven's sake.

Timothy dragged himself onto the highest shelf, surveying the warehouse. He'd never been up here before. Never felt the need. While Felix liked being up high, Timothy liked being on the floor, seeing *who* was coming and going. He liked listening to Dan's stories. It didn't make him a bad cat. He wondered what the creatures, glowing with their green light, confused, strangers out of time, had been like in their former lives. Dan said some of them were beloved pets who'd died naturally, but others—most of them—were sacrificed to an ancient cat goddess. If she'd existed, she'd been lost to time, at least to American cats like Timothy. He studied the creatures below him from his eagle perch. Probably some of them had appreciated their humans and had affection for them, going willingly until they realized what the human was going to do. Some of them likely fought, like Felix would fight. Some of the mummies were plump like Timothy, not all of them svelte and cunning. In the warehouse, in death as in life, possibly, some of them worked to find an escape, some milled around, confused and lost.

Timothy stared down at the barrel, and without giving it more thought, without talking himself out of it, launched himself down. He'd never liked jumping.

Never liked the feeling of free fall. Preferred to pick his way down step by step.

He struck the barrel on its edge, happy for the extra weight he carried, because his target moved, shuddered, tipped. He landed, claws grabbing the wood of the pallet to hold him in place. For a heartbeat, he thought his weight hadn't been enough. That they would be forced to burn.

The barrel slid over the edge. Timothy didn't know how far it was up in the air, but high enough that time slowed as it dropped, falling… falling maybe forever. End over end, rotating in space. He wanted to close his eyes but couldn't allow it.

The metal crashed to the concrete floor of the warehouse, landing on its edge, and splitting open. Chemicals, glowing green, nearly the same color as the magic imbuing the ancient cats, spattered across the room. It sizzled and spit, hissing like the cats it landed on. The eyes winked out one by one throughout the room, reducing the number of antagonists dramatically.

There was collateral damage, too—it couldn't be helped. Some of the other crates and boxes sizzled and melted, but it was a far cry from the total loss of Felix's plan. Timothy hopped down (no more dramatic dives for him) to survey what was left.

It's not getting them all, Felix said. *But it got a lot of them. Can you help me with the rest?* Any praise, coming from Felix, meant a great deal.

Fighting. Timothy wasn't good at… it didn't matter. *Yeah.*

I'll try and leave you the little ones.

Timothy wasn't sure that made him feel better, but he'd take it.

And whatever you do, don't get any of that shit on your feet.

Timothy wanted to be annoyed at the reminder, but it was a kindness. A kindness from someone who struggled to show such emotions.

Thanks, Timothy muttered.

Felix shot into action. Timothy's plan had reduced the number of cat mummies by more than half, from those taken out in the first spattering assault, but the ancient things didn't understand it, some of them wandered into the smoldering puddle. As it ate through the bandages on their paws, the magic depleted. The green drifted away, and the cats collapsed.

Not all of them, though. Some still tried to escape. Timothy saw a smaller cat mummy dart under the shelving, squeezing into the darkness underneath. He followed, dust tickling his whiskers. Being on the floor he was exposed, at the whim of these monsters. He heard Felix's battle yowls but could no longer see his friend. Timothy jutted out a paw and clawed at the escaping mummy's wrapping. His paw soared through air. He had to push himself further under the shelf. The floor pressed into his belly, the shelf into his back. His quarry came up against the back wall and spun around, facing Timothy. Spirals of magic, twisting and pulsating, cosmos of wonder.

What if there was more than the Heaviside Layer? Where was the magic going? It made sense, he told himself, the spirits of the cats went up, up, up to the Heaviside Layer, where all cats belonged.

The mummy howled in his face, and Timothy lashed out, his paw passing through the greenish aura of its eyes. He shuddered, but his claws connected with the linen wrappings. Gaining ground, he lashed out with his other paw too, hissing and spitting. His prey made a sorrowful yowl as the light winked out. Yes! Another one down! Timothy backed carefully out from under the shelves. A weight dropped on his rear end as soon as he was free, pinning his back legs to the cement floor.

The weight pressed on Timothy and a stabbing pain bloomed by the base of his tail. *My spine!* He thrashed and fought to pull himself free, finally pulling his face out from under the shelving. One of the larger cats loomed over him, glaring down with enchanted green eyes.

I can't fight you, he thought, but the thing was on top of him and had already bitten him once. He had to. Timothy used his weight to shove the creature back, to force himself onto it. He reluctantly sank his teeth into the linen wrapping its throat. He used his strong hind legs to dig at the stomach, his claws finding purchase and ripping at the linens. Timothy felt the magic flow out of it, kicking himself free and spitting scraps from his mouth. They didn't taste so bad, and somehow the almost pleasantness made him even more eager to spit them out.

Felix fought dangerously close to the acid. Only a few cats remained. Timothy thought some might be kittens and they succumbed to his attacks. He batted them into the chemicals, bowled them over, each time thinking how sorry he was, how he hoped he was setting them free. By the time he'd taken care of them, Felix stood surveying the now-quiet battleground.

It'll be dawn soon. You should hide. I'm going to bolt when they get here. I don't want them blaming us for this.

The thought never occurred to Timothy. It should have. Once, there was a cat called Mischa, who'd taken to spraying to mark his territory. Dan and Valeria made that cat disappear because he was bad for business.

But we saved them!

I'd still hide, if I were you. And I'm getting out of here until things cool down.

Mechanical beeping filled the warehouse, Dan putting in his code in the lock. Felix ran towards the sound. Timothy wedged himself back under the shelving so he could see.

Dan cried out as he opened the door and Felix blasted out between his legs into the cold. The big cat had puffed his tail and given himself crazy eyes, sprinting away, seeming terrified.

"Holy shit." Dan flicked the overhead lights on, fluorescents buzzing to life, and surveyed the damage: the corner of the mummies' crate even more damaged, acid spattered and running throughout the main work floor and… one hundred dead cats, their mummified bodies desecrated. "Timothy! Tim! Kitty kitty!"

Timothy allowed himself the smallest mew. Dan's head whipped towards him.

"Holy shit, what is all this?" Valeria's voice now.

"I don't know. Felix ran for the hills when I came in. Poor guy was terrified, and I can't find Tim!"

"Is that… Dan, be careful, that's the acid. What happened in here?" Valeria paused. Then took up the calls of "Timothy? Kitty! C'mere, kitty!"

Plastic crinkled. His Greenies. He cried out, the most pitiful meow he could muster (though he was hungry and wanted to get some of those Greenies).

"I hear him." Dan's voice grew closer. "The mummies are all over the place. They're ruined. Tim! They're unwrapped, and in the chemicals, some are under the shelves. What is this? What will the museum say?"

"We need to get cameras installed. Was there an earthquake last night? That barrel was up on the third shelf. It wasn't, like, near the edge or anything." She paused. "How did the mummies get out?"

"I put the barrel up there myself. It was secure. Tim!" Dan's face filled the space in front of Timothy, and he let the human pull him free. He went limp, exhausted, and willing Valeria to come with the Greenies. She marveled at the surrounding destruction.

"He seems okay. He's terrified, though. What did you see last night, buddy? You okay?"

You wouldn't believe me if I told you, Timothy said, nestling into Dan's arms. *One hundred dead cats.*

REANIMATION
CARTER LAPPIN

Mek has already climbed out, brushed himself off, and is sitting on top of the glass display case by the time he hears them come in.

They're different from the last group; younger, and less solemn. He hears them chattering amongst themselves before they're even in the room. "—not sure if the translation is accurate—" A woman is talking, but she cuts off when she sees Mek sitting there.

He waves.

"Hello," he says. Behind the woman, three others gawk. They all look very young—barely into the modern sense of adulthood. Mek takes the amulet from where he's been keeping it in his lap and holds it toward them. "I think you're looking for this."

—

The first time, Mek is pretty sure everyone, including himself, is equally surprised. One moment, Mek is dead, and the next, someone is leaning over him, holding an amulet by the chain, dirt and fear smudged across the stranger's face. They're grave robbers, he'll surmise later, though probably more hungry and scared than they are greedy or evil.

Mek screams, a horrible, roaring sound, and so does the robber. The robber scrambles back, and the amulet slips out of his grasp. Mek has time only to watch it hit the stone floor and shatter, pieces scattering like sand across the desert, and then Mek is alive no longer.

—

The woman is a scholar, she tells him. She'd studied the myths, but she hadn't truly…

"Believed?" Mek finishes for her.

The woman nods. "Yes, I guess so. I suppose I hadn't expected you. The myths all said that you'd be… different. Terrible. Dangerous."

"Perhaps once they would have been right," Mek says.

—

The second time, he is alone. There is nobody to frighten but himself. After he pulls himself together and claws the bandages from his face, Mek looks around.

The robbers hadn't taken much, if anything. The doorway is collapsed in on itself now, not simply sealed. Mek supposes that's the sort of thing one might do if the corpse they were trying to rob suddenly started to fight back. He looks at the carvings and paintings on the wall, all bright colors and storytelling.

It is in this way that Mek discovers his fate. He destroys the amulet himself. Death doesn't last long. It never will.

—

One of the students looks at him with doubt. "You're—"

Mek smiles. "Mek."

The student squints at him, leaning to peer at the plaque. Mek laughs. "My true name is difficult for me to hear you mispronounce. Mek is fine." It is similar to what his brothers called him as a child—a nickname meant to tease, meant to remind him of his youth. Mek is not young any longer, but the name is one he has grown to like. Perhaps names, like everything else, are meant to change with time.

"You're the mummy?" the scholar asks.

—

The next time, Mek tries to get out. He scrabbles and tears at the blocked entrance, tossing aside rocks and dust and stone. He digs too frantically, too quickly. The path he makes collapses in on him. Something must break, because that is the end of that.

———

The scholar puts her arm out to block her students from getting too close to Mek. Protecting them. The lights in the museum are low. Mek thinks he must look like a monster to them.

———

The time after that, he is somewhere else. A wooden room, with Mek's belongings stacked in crates and the history of him forgotten. This time, he is more prepared, but, more importantly, this time, he is angry. He is so angry. There are men around, men who exclaim in surprise when Mek rises with his anger from a crate of his own, men who are soft and pale and carry what Mek will later know to be guns but now only knows how they shout and bite at him.

The men shoot him. Mek kills one of them. He feels sorry about it almost immediately, looking down at the dead man and wondering if it had really been him who did that, if those really had been his hands, his will working toward this end. Perhaps he has been changed more than he realized, or, worse, perhaps he has not changed much at all.

Mek is shot, and the amulet around his neck is broken. Mek is alive no longer. If, indeed, he ever has been.

———

"Yes, I am the mummy. Or perhaps the mummy is me," Mek says. "Once, I thought there might be a difference."

One of the students looks up at this, from where they had been crouched, using a pen to poke at the cloth strips Mek had peeled away from himself like a second skin. When they see Mek looking back, they duck their head, breaking the eye contact.

To the scholar, Mek says, "I thought you'd come soon. Someone usually does."

The scholar is holding a book, annotated heavily where she's been studying it. "According to historical record, the people who excavated your tomb believed you were cursed. Death is said to follow wherever you go."

There's no such thing as curses. Then again, there's no such thing as the dead coming back to life either. Mek says, "I've never known, really, if it was meant to be a curse or a gift. Nobody ever told me."

———

The lid of his stone coffin is easy enough to push aside, but it's been encased in something that's much more difficult to break through.

"It's you," says a trembling man once Mek has made his way out. The bandages around Mek's hand are torn and his fingers twisted, but Mek doesn't feel the pain of it.

Mek tilts his head, only looking.

The man has a gun in his belt. Mek knows what it is now. The man does not touch it, though his hand hovers above it as though it is a snake that might bite. He wears a metal pin on his collar, like, Mek will think later, a religious man might wear a cross. Like it might protect him. Mek knows now what a gun is, and he knows now that he does not like them.

The man says, "My father warned me about you."

"Who," says Mek, "will you warn?"

———

"How is it possible?" asks a student, the one with the pink hair, as Mek climbs off of the display case. The sarcophagus beneath it is a reproduction—what they believe his might once have looked like. They are wrong. Mek is not sorry for it. This one has wonderful colors. "I mean, we translated the writing on your tomb—"

Mek hadn't known they found his resting place once again. He thinks he might miss it. It was quiet there. He doesn't know how to feel knowing that these people have seen it, have read what was painted on the walls of it so long ago. Have seen the fallen torches where the grave robbers scrambled to escape him so many lifetimes past, have felt the fear that lingered there. Have seen what death could have been for Mek had things been different.

"We know that you're supposed to wake every so often, and that the amulet is what ties you to life. But *how?* Is it magic?" the student continues.

"Maybe it is," Mek says. "Maybe someone loved me. Maybe someone hated me."

***

Mek is alone. He's in a warehouse, he determines. The side of his resting place is tagged with a strange seal. He thinks he recognizes it from the metal pin the last man wore.

Mek climbs out.

There is much to see. Mek wanders for a while. He does not kill anyone. He thinks, perhaps, this time, life may stick.

A man finds Mek in the library. He is wearing the same pin. He knows to go for the amulet.

***

"There was a cult," the scholar says, "dedicated to stopping your rise. For generations members passed down the legend of an evil pharaoh who would stop at nothing to bring back his rule. We studied some of their notes. They're part of what brought us here today."

Mek hadn't been anyone special. Only rich enough for a tomb. His family would have wanted him to have a good afterlife. "I never knew any pharaohs," he says.

———

Mek wakes behind glass. He gets one hand up, spider-webbing cracks blooming to life across the display's clear surface.

This time, there are no more pins, but there is a man, and the man does not wait for Mek to catch his bearings, to blink, to cough the dust from lungs that have not been used in a long time.

The man shatters the glass himself, but the end result is the same. Mek greets death, but death does not pay him the same courtesy. Not for long, at least.

———

"I think…" says the scholar, sitting next to him. She has sent her students off on some task, and the two of them are alone. "That your reanimations have something to do with the positioning of the stars, or maybe the passing of a comet through the skies. Do you know how many years it was between awakenings?"

"Less and less, I think," Mek says. "You came because you heard of the curse?"

"I translated the writing in your tomb. I did the research. I thought we might have to stop you."

"I thought you might, too." Mek pauses. "What was it like? My tomb?"

She pauses too. "Empty. Beautiful. I think it would have been nice to rest there."

"Yeah. Me too."

———

He only ever seems to wake at night. The security guards are the ones to catch him this time. Someone, it appears, has warned them about him.

Mek escapes to the painting wing to look at the art there. The security guards don't know about the amulet, don't know that to break it will be to end this terrifying night. So when their nightsticks and the knives from a civilization almost as old as Mek don't work, they get innovative.

In want of another option, they come at him from both sides. Their stun guns pierce into Mek; hooking barbs with wires that jolt. They hold the triggers down until Mek shakes and shakes and the ancient linens wrapped around Mek finally catch and spark. Mek can feel himself crackling, can almost smell the electricity and the pain.

The amulet melts this time.

———

He passes the scholar the amulet. "It doesn't matter how thoroughly it's destroyed. It always comes back. So do I."

She turns it over in her hands. "I'm sorry."

"Will you point at the stars? The ones whose movement my life follows."

The scholar hesitates, like she knows what Mek means, knows what Mek is going to ask of her. Knows what to do with the amulet she has cradled in her hand. Knows that she will, in the end, do it for him anyways.

She says, "I don't have to break it. Not yet. There's much we can learn from each other."

"That's alright," Mek says. "But if the next time I awaken is soon, will you try to be there?"

"I will."

———

The amulet breaks.

PAINTED AS A VILLAIN

MORGAN WEST-BURNHAM

This is not the world that I left.

There is a man here, pale and nervous. He paints. He stares into a little shining square, perhaps a mirror for scrying or tool of divination, but it often distresses him. He snaps off limbs from the others like me, grinding them into a fine dust for his purposes. Soon, I'll be next.

———

"I promise, your client will be thrilled with the condition," Nicolas says loudly, tilting his head to his cellphone where it sits on his easel on speaker. He compares the image on the screen to the canvas in front of him, eyes narrow.

Another voice replies through the phone amidst the background rush of traffic, "They were really happy with the last one, and she's reaching out to her friends. There are a lot of collectors looking for some of these specific pieces."

"New Age Pagans and Spiritualists?" Nicolas asks, dragging his brush gently across the canvas.

"Exactly. They love a taste of antiquity, especially if there's something morbid and dead wrapped up in it. I'm heading to her office now, so I'll get back to you soon if I hear of anyone interested in the remaining pieces."

"Bye," Nicolas mumbles, waiting for the call to disconnect before allowing himself a heavy sigh.

It's fine, he thinks. *It's good to get rid of them fast.* He takes a deep breath, trying to quell the sudden, panicked throb of his heart. *I can stall for time.*

He had promised the art dealer a half dozen paintings; there were only so many unaccounted pieces from Burne-Jones and Drölling and that seemed a safe number. But he had also said he had possession of them all—a fortunate find in a poorly overseen estate sale— though he had not yet finished painting them.

His studio is flushed bright with sunlight through the high windows. The place is a mess, with his unmade cot set up in the far corner, crumbs surrounding the hotplate on the table shoved beside the deep basin sink, and workbench covered in the dust and detritus more befitting an archeology department than an artist's studio. His eyes skim over this workbench and, feeling again the throb of panic, he closes them.

Nicolas has done a bad thing.

—

The man comes and goes. Sometimes with one of his paintings, carefully wrapped. Around me are the broken shapes of my fellows: small sarcophagi smashed open, stiff wrappings coiled around like snake skins, and the snarling, sleeping faces.

He keeps snapping bits off at a time, but he always saves the head for last. He must feel guilty. Or afraid. I wish I could wake up back in the dreamy Field of Reeds, prowling with Bastet and laying on the sun-soaked sands by the river's bank.

The man seems nervous, but not unhappy. He keeps staring into that shining square and it throws lights onto the walls that I cannot chase. I wonder if he sees the future written on its surface.

—

The process for making the paint is an evolving one, he keeps telling himself. Nicolas had felt confident in his ability to match hues and he had mixed plenty of paint before.

His first attempts with the food processor are a botch, the paint coming out clumpy and thin, more of a vacuous taupe. He curses at himself for the waste of materials.

The next attempt, he's more careful. It was enough of a challenge to smuggle what he did out of the museum, with the storage for the Egyptian exhibits on the far end from his own workspace in restorations. He couldn't afford to take anything else.

This time, he grinds the bits by hand.

The resulting shades are luminously rich, imbued with a glow of warmth.

Nicolas presses a brush into the paint, then touches it to the prepared canvas. There's a gleam to the hue. He smiles.

Creating forgeries is a challenge he enjoys. Working in restoration, the process is focused on nursing a piece back to its original state as much as possible. But in this endeavor, he works against his professional impulse. He artifices the effects of time.

He spends months preparing his forgeries, claiming two as unaccounted for paintings of the artists Edward Burne-Jones and Martin Dröller, as well as several supposedly unknown pieces, which affords him a little creative freedom.

Nicolas' world shifts to his studio and his work. There's too much to finish: documents to show a paper trail, receipts from the alleged estate sale, aging on the finished pieces, grinding the remaining materials into the last of the paints.

Outside, the cars streak past, tires hissing in the rain, while Nicolas works, sweating from the powerful lamps turned on to coax the fresh oils to dry. He sits back from his work, packing away the small sarcophagi to be thrown out in stages across different dumpsters around the city. In the corner of his eye, he sees something streak past, a gray smudge disappearing around his cot.

He stands, dusting his hands off on his jeans. Nothing moves on that side of the studio.

Crash.

He turns, eyes darting to catch the source of the noise, but it's only a thick-bottomed glass, falling unbroken on the cement floor. His orange cat sits on the ledge where the glass had been, peering at him.

"Dammit, Toulouse." Nicolas pushes the incriminating trash aside, skin prickling with guilt.

———

"I'm just so impressed that you found these in such good condition!" she exclaims, giving Nicolas' upper arm a gentle squeeze.

He laughs in what he hopes is a confident, casual way and takes a step away from the painting where it hangs in its new home. "Well, I got lucky at an estate sale. They didn't know what they had."

She nods, moving closer to the painting, studying it. "And this is one of the ones he used the actual mummy brown pigment in? Like, the *actual* mummy paint?"

"It is," he says, sticking his hands in his pockets. "Not many survived. It's said that when he found out how they made the paint, he ordered a burial of any of his works that used that pigment."

"No! A burial? For the paintings themselves?"

"That's what they say." His phone buzzes in his pocket and he holds up a finger, stepping away into the corridor.

A text from his landlord.

Strange sounds coming from his apartment, like cats scratching and yowling at the door.

He frowns. Toulouse has always been a quiet cat. *I wonder what's gotten into him.* He taps out a short reply and returns to find the art dealer investigating an edge.

He clears his throat and she turns, smiling.

"It really is a beautiful piece; my client will be really pleased," she says, sauntering back toward him. "Just because I'm sure it's going to come up, did you do any, ah, restorative touches to the piece?"

He stares at her, his mind bursting into panic, "What? Of course not. Why would you—"

"Only because you work in restoration, of course!" she cuts him off, reaching her fingertips out to smooth his lapels. "No need to get nervous." She tilts her head, smiling, her eyes narrow.

"Oh, yeah. Of course. If I were to touch up a piece, I would reveal that before anyone made a purchase. Trust me."

———

There isn't much of me left. I remember the feel of my limbs in life, strong and powerful, wrapped gently at the end to keep me safe in the journey to the fields and Bastet. But I can't feel anything now. I hear my companions, the others like me, stirring nearby. Their bodies have all been gone for some days. I think I'm the last.

The man seems on edge. I haven't seen him sleeping. He avoids answering his door. I know he will come for the rest of me before long.

———

He wakes to the pressure of something heavy on his chest. It feels as if the weight is constricting his lungs, tightening with each exhale so he gets a little less air in the next breath. The studio is still dark. Through the window streaks shades of soft lavender and gray, heralding early morning and a sun not yet risen. Nicolas tries to move his arms to push the weight off his chest. It must be Toulouse.

His arms don't move.

He struggles, but his body does nothing.

His eyes dart around the dim apartment. At the foot of the cot, Toulouse is stretching slowly, pink mouth widened in a sharp yawn.

Nicolas tries to take a deep breath, and feels the wind being pressed out of him. The thing on his chest stirs.

It shifts, uncoiling itself and turning, pressing small feet into his sternum as it sits upright, tucking its tail along its legs and peering down at him with slitted, green eyes.

A cat, but not his.

He struggles to move again, but he can't do more than twitch his fingers.

The cat stares down at him, unblinking, then rises slowly into an arch as its face contorts and lips snarl back from its teeth. It hisses.

Nicolas manages to scream. The sound unlocks his limbs and he sits up, flailing wildly, hitting himself in his chest as he jumps from his cot. But there's only Toulouse, scampering away with a puffed-up tail, turning round eyes reproachfully back on him.

Rubbing his chest, Nicolas shakes his head and fumbles on the makeshift nightstand for his phone, pulling it from the charger.

Twelve missed messages, four of them calls.

He swipes the screen and scrolls through the texts: all of them asking for him to call, to answer a question from a client about the quality of a particular, previously lost piece. His cheeks feel cool as the blood drains from his face, and he sits back down on the edge of the cot.

He's caught, or he's cursed.

He looks at the workbench with the dust and remnants of the mummies he had used for his pigments.

They're everywhere.

At first, Nicolas could explain the flitting shadows as Toulouse, sprinting around the studio, but now he sees them everywhere: sitting on every ledge and shelf, slinking underneath his cot, disappearing around a corner. He even sees them outside, glimpses of cats sitting in the alleyways or darting into traffic as he rushes down the sidewalk, his head down against the battering rain.

They're following me, he thinks wildly.

He finds himself back in the office with the art dealer. She isn't touching his arm this time.

She levels her blue eyes at him, her lips pulling a gentle frown. "I'm not sure what you're asking for."

"I need the painting back," Nicolas stammers, standing rain-soaked and wringing his hands in the hallway. "I know your client had some concerns—"

She laughs. "You haven't addressed any of them! She's worried the painting is stolen, and you want to take it back, what, to try and sell it to someone else? I don't think so."

He feels a momentary, shocking flutter of pride in himself that his work would be mistaken for theft before forgery, but it is drowned out swiftly as he catches a creeping shadow in the corner of his vision.

"I can assure her that the painting is not stolen," he sputters, struggling not to turn his head to search for the shadows. "I just need to match it with the... appropriate documentation."

She shakes her head. "I don't think so. You need to leave."

Nicolas hisses out a curse and gives in, turning his head. The shadow appears as a cat sitting perfectly still, watching him with the cold appraisal of a long-dead god. A shudder runs through him and he jerks his head back to her. "I can't do that."

Nicolas pushes past her, more roughly than he intended, and she stumbles back into the wall. His wet shoes slap on the tiled floor as he runs down the hall, turning into the room where he had helped to hang the painting. He rips it off the wall, holding it awkwardly under one arm as he runs back down the way he came.

"Hey!" she shouts after him, watching as he tears through the front door and disappears into the sheets of rain.

—

The studio goes dark, the massive lights hanging from the rafters suddenly extinguished. Lights from outside, cutting slowly through the ropes of rain over the paned windows, flash and quaver on the walls, but cannot penetrate the depths.

He tries using the light on his phone, shaking it side to side to trigger the device, but it won't toggle on. He swears and smacks the phone against the flat of his hand, shaking it again.

Nothing.

He sees shapes wending through the gray. The pale, hollow flicker of lantern-eyes, shining green in the dim.

First, he only sees one set. Just Toulouse, perhaps.

But then other pairs spring from the blackness. Shining dimly his way.

Soon, he's cornered by more than a dozen glowing sets of eyes, all fixed on him. There's a low thrumming of growls gathering deep in feline throats. He backs away, cornered in the studio space.

Knocking over an easel and its drying oil canvas, he knows what he must do. There are no more remains left to bury, unless he can scrape together enough discarded dust from his efforts. No paint remains either, except for what he laid into the canvas. He picks up the fallen painting and throws it into the middle of the studio space, a barrier between him and the eyes of the cats peering out of gray, statuesque forms. He gathers the other paintings, the ones he reclaimed and repossessed and the ones not yet sold, and casts them into the center as well.

The ghostly shapes of the cats watch on as he splashes turpentine over the pile.

He throws a match onto it.

The flames blossom rapidly, fueled by the fumes of the chemicals, and then turn to devour the canvas and wood.

In the sudden flash of light, Nicolas has to squeeze his eyes shut, but he pries his lids open to watch the flames consume the paintings. Around the fire, the shimmering glow of the eyes still watch him, closer than they had been before.

He feels the sweat dripping from his brow. Behind, he hears a terrible yowl as the cats around him begin to grow and arch and hiss, their eyes fire.

There's the sudden impact of sharp, curved claws digging into his back.

He reaches up and behind him, trying to pry the cat off, but it sinks its claws in deeper, cutting jaggedly through his skin as he pulls. Another cat pounces and latches its claws into his thigh, and another into his thrashing arm. Like a pride of diminutive lions, they dig in and hold, bringing him to the ground in a bleeding, weeping mess.

The flames roar as the cats swarm him. His own Toulouse swipes at his eyes. And Nicolas sees no more.

IN MY LITTLE, DEAD WAY

JENNIFER LESH FLECK

We were discovered together in this 1900s ware-house that was once home to a cheesemaking enterprise—its ghost sign faintly visible on the brick exterior, a mural of a wild-eyed rat caught in the claws of a top-hatted, monocled cat with a madman's grin. Inside was the unmistakable pungency of old dairy products, a confusing funk permeating scarred floors and whitewashed walls. Taxes were overdue on the property. There'd been long-standing confusion and dispute over its ownership. The windows were soaped over, and yellowed paperwork left strewn everywhere, like someone departed in great haste.

Copies of an obscure contract for services rendered a decade prior.

Seventeen giant glass pickling vats sat on steel shelving, each containing the remains of one singular, privileged individual.

Our corpses were folded like we'd been preparing to be shot from cannons into the boundless ether: arms pressed to chests, knees tucked under chins. Liters of honey had been poured in, bathing us. As *DailyMail.com* proclaimed, our bodies laid out on tarps and plastic sheeting were, "strikingly well-preserved, if rather sticky and jaundiced-looking." We'd all died before the processing part happened. The mellification, the mummifying of our remains. Many of us were bald or nearly bald, all of us scrawny and wasted from some terminal state or another.

The viscous fluid itself possessed various amber and straw hues, depending on what had been in season— clover, alfalfa, linden tree, ragweed. In that infamous group photo, our vats look like a collection of giant piss samples.

We were all formerly missing people: minor tech scions, more than one B-grade actor, a well-known comedian. Random rich-but-not-endlessly-wealthy personalities who'd been backed into some mortal corner or another. We'd wanted to hit pause on death. The big promise, of course, being our eventual resuscitations.

A restart in some better world.

I don't know… listen. I was in stage 4 colorectal cancer when I digitally signed on the dotted line.

We each paid two prices to be mellified. First, $59K-162K in either unmarked bills or untraceable cryptocurrency for the process, which included a brief stay in a private hospice center and transport, post-mortem, to the cheesery.

The second cost of entry was more abstract but arguably more difficult to handle: we were forbidden to visit anyone during our hospice respite. We could tell no one. We'd die among strangers, become members of that vast, mysterious club, "The Missing."

Found on a low shelf—my glass vat extra dusty—was me, Lana De'lonzo. A one-time Instagram influencer called "OldMoneyBlonde" with, at last count, 1.8m followers. I was a self-proclaimed "chic maxi-minimalist." My hair color was dishwater, rebranded. The implied reference to institutional, hoarded wealth? A myth.

Before I died, strangers peered at my colorful, well-filtered images and videos. Endless footage of primped scenes, all the mess pushed outside the frame.

They looked at *me* and dreamed.

Colorectal disease is painful, messy, *unsexy*. Real shitty, that'd be accurate. I considered a comeback, an earnest pivot towards indomitable spirit and "Brave Cancer Warrior." That niche was chock-a-block full. I found no creative way to romanticize certain things. Like the morning an Art Nouveau sterling silver hair clip slid loose and hit the Carrera countertop, *tink-tink*.

I stopped posting, my death arriving shortly before the second surgery could be scheduled, the one involving a stoma, a bag fitted to it.

I disappeared. No goodbyes.

My twin sister Maude shows up the day after Memorial Day to identify my remains.

Poor Maude!

Born identical twins, we had mirror-level DNA. But certain epigenetic influences had not been equally kind. Early on, she turned sly, peevish, and private, while I flowered into the extrovert, the "pretty sister."

Dear Maude, fast approaching middle age, sniffly from May pollens. She stares at my naked, sticky form left splayed on the morgue table, no trace of rigor mortis. "Oh yeah, that's her. That's my darling Lana."

Some consciousness in my sweetened brain awakens, improbably turning toward her voice, groping like a neglected houseplant when sunlight finally appears. A Swiss Cheese Monstera, I like to think.

Something arty and hip.

Laws changed during the decade I slumbered, becoming all loosey-goosey.

What would've been inconceivable and unconscionable is now both permissible and largely overlooked, former costly resources funneled away elsewhere. Once it's been determined there is no detectable foul play, law and legal enforcers are happy to release "organic and/or associated/related evidence" to loved ones to dispose of on their own dime.

Maude arrives the day after Labor Day to collect my remains. "It's in preparation for a gathering—something special," she says, her smile demure and loopy, her eyes glossy with tears. She hulks there with her gut out in polyester slacks covered in pet hair. "I'll take that giant pickle jar and the glop in it, too. Better than just dumping it."

Now here we are, the De'lonzo Twins, in Maude's home after over two decades apart. I'm stuffed in my vat of honey, upside down as before, my senses slowly, foggily returning. Murky, like the bottom of some swamp, veiled by leaf rot and tannins, but tasting sugar. I've tried to move my tongue to speak, but I'm paralyzed.

Some of my new sensory input, I'm experiencing *through* my sister. I use Maude like I once used my iPhone Pro to magnify instructions on a bottle of Xeloda. Little zoomed-in sips of her world, and I'm *so* greedy for them.

Maude's "house" is a basement hovel stuffed with musty furniture and yarn-based blankets. The creaks and thuds on the popcorn ceiling with its breast-shaped light offer hints of mysterious dramas acted out elsewhere. Mean little windows allow in a chaotic early September light through busted plastic blinds.

Maude's got three orange-striped cats, more feral than friendly. One skinny poodle mix, its murky eyes staining mushroom-colored curls. The dog barks at the slightest of noises, its whole body trembling.

This mongrel sniffs my vat.

Boo-yeah! I yell inside my head. Its matted hackles rise, and it holds itself stiffly, rebuffed and offended. The yapping begins anew.

So I *do* still have some influence beyond the glass. In my little, dead way.

Maude says, "Ah, BonBon! Meet my older sis, Lana."

By exactly two minutes, I'm her senior. Even now, I hold onto that shit like it means something.

———

Maude revived OldMoneyBlonde!

I can hardly believe it, but I suppose my Instagram password is easily cracked (our mother's maiden name + our birth year, a choice I'd made glibly, a private joke).

> Heeeeeyyyy, long time no post. Maude here, Lana's twin. As many of you are aware, Lana's been found! Not really alive, but v well preserved. She's livin la vida loca right here w me in my lil casita. Updates 4th-coming!!1

A flood of hearts are quickly appended to that post. Twenty-two comments, congratulatory, sympathetic, and wildly, inappropriately curious.

The photo she's chosen to reveal? My jar, taken using the flash on her crap phone. The glass reflects the dim, cluttered room. Inside, a skeleton with amber skin and a froggishly bloated belly, chemo'd hair plastered across my smooshed-to-the-glass cheek that I want, super badly, to style better. It's like something you'd encounter in the Mütter Museum in some alcove near the exit, the exact spot where everybody's already had their perverse curiosities satisfied.

All those years of careful curation, then the big step I took towards eternal preservation! Only to have my goddamn biggest account reawakened like this.

With one photo, she's ruined my account's aesthetic. Countless photos of French casement windows, open, with flowing cream silk drapes. An antique book shot at a creative angle, a perfect autumn leaf against a stark blue October sky, a puddle reflecting my slender feet in red designer leather. My final image? A pistachio maca-ron on a Wedgwood plate, my hand poised to one side. I'm wearing an antique scarab ring. Already becoming rags draped over bones—my skin prematurely loose and slide-y. It took me an hour's extra work to fiddle it all into a good look.

I scream at Maude in my head.

A tabby cat yowls and swats at thin air. BonBon sniffs, then lifts his leg on my vat, no longer threatened.

Maude, bundled in a puke-green knit on her futon, smiles wistfully. Registering nothing of a fury that burns so hot, this honey should be boiling. She gnaws a piece of fingernail away, flicks it into the hinterlands, and pokes at her crappy phone some more.

Answering my fans, their insipid, predictable questions.

A week, and she's gone and changed shit on me, the bitch. No longer am I OldMoneyBlonde, but OldHoneyMummy!

I'd lost followers in the ten years I was missing, sure. Creative entropy and account neglect fucks you up algorithmically. There's an art to posting with military regularity—hell, all my posts were coordinated to automatically drop to coincide with my core demographic's peak activity.

That bland, pathetic macaron-and-death-hand pic had sickened me, to be truthful. I hated ending on *that* note. It didn't add to the "social conversation." I'd abandoned my life's work to, what, become a layabout in some secret ward located in McFarland, California? That stretch of Interstate 99 is infamous for its buffet of agribusiness emissions—all stripes of pungent and foul. McFarland, in particular. A reek like manure and spoiled grapes, fields of it burning unchecked in hell, forever. I'd collapsed at eternity's padlocked gate—and that's what I get? I died alone, clutching a damp, sour pillow without a case. My legacy? Becoming a specimen in a dusty fromagerie.

Good ol' Maude, though. She's chipper AF, arriving home to chortle at her pets and kick off sweaty boots and pull on pilly pajamas. She chows down on a Hungry Man chicken dinner, scrolling and poking, greasing up the screen. Teary-eyed behind smudged glasses, her gaze full of unearned pride. I take voyeuristic sips of her sad little life from my sad little death, peeking over her shoulder.

I'd assumed OldHoneyMummy might momentarily swell with activity, the name change a novelty—sparking only to flatline. It takes skill to run this shiz. She lacks the experience needed to maintain an account of my caliber. Her halo effect is temporary at best, this twin of someone truly luminary. Maude doesn't have my "special sauce."

Followers are endlessly ravenous for new content, but immediately bored of it, too. It floats before their retinas, and they're already fidgeting, ready to bounce. You gotta hook those eyes, Maude—sink it in the jelly. Haul that slippery catch aboard your sloppy sloop! Lift those nets and bash the fishies' heads before they wriggle overboard. Throw out the bots and worthless bycatch, and slap those prized followers on ice.

If you're monetized, consistent, and your niche remains mesmerized, the ducats and the doubloons pour in.

Ha-ha, poor Maude. They're leaving already—fleas streaming from a boring, dead thing wearing furry slippers and an ugly frown.

Maybe it's harsh, maybe it's mean. But I'm pleased as punch. Loyalty's a cheap farce—if I can't have my people, well, neither can she.

For a while, Maude's a glum dummy, slouching around all sour and lost.

She swipes right on a hot woman out of her league—and gets ghosted for the Halloween party. Something-something happens at work/with work, and she's up till 4 a.m. writing an overdue report, sweaty, slamming Red Bull Zeros ("Now with Monkfruit!"), conned into being somebody's mule again.

Then, out of the actual blue, our poor, put-upon girl's up and at 'em again.

New day, new scheme. Maude 3.0.

She breezes in with an air of clumsily brisk purpose to set up an ersatz studio. Cheap mic, her phone positioned using cereal boxes, ffs. She's ditched the glasses, flimsy ring light filling her eyes with Os. Plopped a wig on, a platinum moppet-cut like young Natalie Portman in *The Professional*. I don't *get* the aesthetic she's chasing—it's loopy and discordant—but I'm fascinated.

This murky half-life is boring.

Maude maneuvers my vat onto a child's plastic wagon—grunting, kvetching—and positions this beside a gaming chair, so I'm sitting shotgun upside-down.

Soon she's doing this streaming press conference, of sorts. The platform's something like Twitch, but like… the latest and greatest. Frankly, I'm surprised. Maude navigates the tech fairly savvily, clickety-clacking the keyboard, performing with a certain confidence, a verve. A sad trickle of watchers soon swells into a small crowd. Her warbling voice settles, becomes strong and measured as she winds herself up to get to the meat.

"Welcome, welcome, Honeybees! For those brand-new to this unusual journey—well, as ever I'm Maude, twin to late influencer Lana De'lonzo, now known as the Honey Mummy…" A chuckle and toss of her head, the blonde wig stiff and unmoving.

What the actual.

"Today I offer you peeps a special opportunity. For $29.95 per bespoke, carefully measured ampule—Venmo or PayPal Friends n' family, please—you'll sample this mysterious, miraculous fluid right here." She pats the lid of my vat. "It's given my big sis a solid decade of quiet dignity, helping her resist rot, degradation, and other gross stuff. It's honey, kids. A special kind found nowhere else. Naturally microbial with an acidic PH. Ingest a spoonful to balance your body. Ol' Herodotus told us how this liquid gold preserved Persian royalty, before *and* after death! Supplement your morning brew. Slather it on—it's a luxuriant topical. I've been taking it for one week already. The glow and benefits, as you can see, are clear and visible."

Maude's lying to them like a damn snake.

"… come on, everyone—let's get mellified! What d'ya got to lose? My Hive finds life more sweet…"

Like some sideshow huckster, my sister rattles brightly into the night, showcasing a zesty intelligence I've never before witnessed. I hang out next to her, cheek smooshed to glass, thinking *no, no, a thousand times n-o…*

Her "initial batch" sells out within the hour.

———

She plunges and dips into my cramped space. Clutching the vat's sticky rim with a blue rubber glove, sucking my sacred honey into a turkey baster, the fluid thick but silky, free of crystals and clouding.

Humming happily, her newly upgraded human hair wig falling around rouged cheeks—a look that, once filtered, somehow becomes something her audience aspires to become.

While she's off doing her livestream, I push into the minds of her cats and her ratdog, scrabble around inside their skulls, getting them agitated. The tabbies yowl and gnaw at paws and flanks. BonBon scoots his bottom on the rug, plagued by imaginary worms. Maude ignores the clamor. She's impervious, locked against my picking and prying. Her new hair's not borrowed keratin but burnished steel—a glorious helm my sister wears, making endless victory laps at some imaginary joust.

I've peeked over her shoulder, seen the swelling numbers. Maude has free Priority Mail packaging stacked ceiling-high. She's got thoughtfully-designed (via her task rabbit from Bangladesh) logo stickers. Branded French ribbon, silk baggies for her ampules. AI assistants, bots spreading her word far and wide.

I flash to a core memory.

Kool-Aid stand, age ten.

I was the darling of the block in my cropped pink gingham, peddling cup after Dixie Cup of faintly sweet, red-dyed swill. We'd watered our precious powder down to extend it beyond normal limits, Maude's idea. She stood behind me at the table, handling all the dirty dollars and quarters. Her punch-pink upper lip with its peach fuzz sparkling in the sun.

Her eyes fixed on me.

With admiration, I figured. Because I had It. Magnetism, charisma, star power—all names for the same ineffable thing. Instinctively I could entrance, command, sell, and sell out.

This quietly simmering thing next to me? I paid her little mind. Her greasy forehead corrugated with nascent worry lines, pebbled by zits. Soon enough the stereotypical bad glasses arrived. Mom popped for extended-wear Acuvue Oasys for me, patiently demonstrating the regimen. You can't blame Mom. I was easier to love.

The dividing fork in the road came on schedule.

"Godspeed, dear Maudie ol' girl," I said years later. "Good luck with… Downtown City College, is it? See ya, can't take ya with me, wish I could, sorry!" Air-kissing a spot near her crusty ear, my hip cocked towards escape.

The horizon glimmered out there, a psychedelic double rainbow as gateway. It all stayed put just long enough for me to breathlessly arrive.

———

My scrawny hips hit the air as the honey level drops, my skin turning bad apple colors.

Maude dips and scoops. Naturally a pragmatist, she never takes any for herself. She knows not to pilfer from her own snake oil, not when it sells for even more as the supply wanes. She's got my vat decorated with

LED lights, displayed for her audience on a motorized turntable, my twisted pelvis oxidizing in the muggy air, becoming yellowed jerky.

It hits at a cellular level, these degrading processes happening fast. Drying out in some spots, liquifying in others. A confusion of chyme from my last meal and other internal goo runs together like a shattered, rotten egg.

If ever I had the faintest hope of coming out alive, it's departing.

"Alive." It means only spirit, not flesh. That's it. That's the big, tough, final takeaway.

This grim news settles, sinking to my heart, the organ now squatting in the heavy broth pooling in my ribcage and filling my clavicles.

—

On Thanksgiving Eve my sister scarfs down Stove Top stuffing and jiggly canned cranberries.

Shortly after wiping her mouth on her t-shirt, Maude hits bottom.

She scrapes at the glass near my nose using a spoon, frowning in her frazzled Warholian wig, whimpering softly. Then lets forth a diarrhetic stream, something like "fuckshitbitchwhoredoggonemuthafucker." BonBon yaps. The tabbies squeeze together under the slumpy couch. Maude's gearing up to climb in beside my wasting corpse to search for traces of product, her desperation a cloud of gnats.

I'm thinking, *Please do, sister. Do.*

Something wicked's come to me. One final gamble I can wing out into the universe like sticky, loaded dice.

I'm thinking, *Come an' get me, you wacky bat. Take it, take it all. Use me as thou wilt, you utterly unbearable wretch.*

Maude abruptly stops the sniveling and the shit-talking. Takes a shuddery, snotty breath and squares those shoulders. She changes into a fresh, cute pumpkin-colored blouse and neatens her wig. Then yanks at my hips with nitrile-gloved fingers, hauling the sloshy ruin of me out. She struggles posing my floppy mummy on an office chair beside her throne, eventually propping Harlequin paperbacks in critical areas. My wasted thighs are now supported by ripped bodices and bulging, bronzed chests.

She goes live.

"Happy, happy Turkey Day, Honeybees. Hope y'all had a good one!" Her voice sounds husky, mirthful, slightly acrid. "Tonight—boy—do I gotta *real* special deal for you! That's right, loves—something unique, coveted, and super rare. For only $99.95, you can get a piece of the original Honey Mummy herself. You heard me correctly. I'm breakin' her down and shippin' her out, kids, and it's all happening tonight. Show up at dawn and you're too late, sorry! Let's see you light up my Venmo, my Zelle, my PayPal right now. I wanna see a traffic jam, friends. A scramble, a skirmish in my inbox, a Doorbuster Friday! You how Miss Maude rolls…" Ring light floods her eyes as she leans forward. "Pro-tip, yeah?" Her voice becomes a whisper. "Listen close, Hive, for the hack. First ones in get the choicest bits! You understand?!"

She's magnificent, Maude is. She leaps from her gaming throne to hip-check me, and my wheeled chair slides out of the frame. "Ever wanted a talisman or totem, a bauble, a bone? Somethin' pretty for the rear-view mirror? Magic token for yer sweetheart? A spoiled secret in your pocket? Well! Then! Get in NOW or get left behind—"

Her eyes bulge as she barks into the darkness, spittle flying. And you know what? I'm proud of her, my Maude. Taking my little dead sips, watching her fall apart. She does it grandly, eccentrically, inimitably. The wig twisted to one side. Her jugular a jumping worm.

Oh, there you are. My dear baby sister. My twin.

———

So this is how it happens. How my spirit busts out of that shitty basement apartment and into your big, wide world once more.

After logging off, Maude throws an apron over her pumpkin top, then breaks me down to the last knucklebone, nail, and tendon. Every bit of me, Maude seals up tightly, slapping on a printed label. Finally she sinks down to a crouch and pets BonBon and the kitties. Closes her eyes, slides comfortably back into her own frowziness—helplessly, gratefully—as dawn steals in.

They zip everywhere, expedited, these boxes of little dead me. Each insured against loss and theft and other untoward circumstances. So I make it safely into brand-new homes across the globe. Opened by trembling hands, my earlobe or molar or scrap of ass-hide stared at with utter disbelief. Can it really be real, be here, be theirs and theirs alone?

It's Independence Day come months and months early. It's come just for me!

They're logging on now.

They're sharing me everywhere, grinning big, loopy grins. So sweet, these firework bursts of awe and excitement. This spreading, stinking smoke—of pride, of ownership—drifting out and out and out.

ROT

RAY DECHANT

The stage door of the opera house swings open, and the casting director emerges, searching for the next name on the clipboard. I tense my legs, trying to keep them from shaking.

"… Jake Wagner?"

I give a weak wave and follow her, gripping my sheet music. The powder I've just dissolved under my tongue leaves a salty, unpleasantly meaty taste in my mouth. I kick myself for how reckless this is: it's stupid to swallow anything unfamiliar before an audition. And yet, some unholy mix of my roommate's rich-girl unflappability and my own desperation convinced me this would give me the edge I needed.

The Victorians were suuuper into this shit, Orchid drawled, passing me a spice jar filled with black powder in between drags of her cigarette. *All the incredible visionaries that came out of that era? Yeah. The pharaohs were part god, y'know?*

I hand my music to the accompanist, then nestle into the bentside of the grand piano, gripping it in the hopes that the casting director won't see my trembling. The Carolan Opera House is no Metropolitan Opera, but even the small parts pay well. I would be fine just putting a chorus role on my resume. After all, Gordon's waiting room warm-ups sounded incredible; he practically had the role of Verdi's MacBeth in the bag.

The accompanist nods and launches into the introductory bars of my audition piece. The director and casting director scratch notes onto a clipboard. I wait, wondering if the old theater superstitions that *MacBeth* is a cursed production extend to auditions. What if this stupid powder dries out my vocal cords or damages them? All I can do now is breathe to my diaphragm, like I've done a million times before.

And the powder hits.

The sound that comes out of me is ethereal. The music pours out of my body and swirls around the air, honeyed and hazy, as if the song wants nothing more than to caress every ear in the room like a lover. The director's eyes snap up to me, his brows rising faintly upwards; the casting director's mouth falls open.

I'm warm all over, and my skin is tingling. I want to bask in their awe and admiration like a stage light. Distantly, some wrongness is nagging at the back of my head, but it doesn't matter. This must be how sunlight feels as it hits a rushing waterfall. It's exhilarating.

Sixteen bars later, my final notes linger in the air, a blown-out candle.

"Callbacks are on Thursday," says the director diplomatically. "We'll post the list tomorrow."

Part god, indeed, I think, as I stride out the door, wondering if success tastes like powdered mummy.

———

"So, do you know how it works?" I ask Orchid as she pours steaming water over the fresh-ground coffee in her pour-over.

Orchid frowns, leaning back on the counter. "I think there's something about, like, consuming the embodiment of the afterlife that raises your vibrations. It's like communing with the ancient muses. Y'know?"

"For sure." I nod automatically. "But what's it like for you afterwards?"

She eyes me. "What do you mean?"

I don't want to tell her about the dreams. Orchid would insist on interpreting them. But I've taken the powdered mummy twice now, once before the audition and once before callbacks, and both times woke up in the dark with sweat drenching the covers and a knot gripping my chest, unable to get back to sleep. In the one last night, I'd pushed a woman off of a temple statue, then watched, remorseless and vaguely curious, as her scream disappeared into the night.

"I don't know," I try to sound casual. "Does dried pharaoh have side effects?"

"Dried mummy," she corrects. "Not every mummy was a pharaoh. And I haven't used it enough to notice much. I got kinda bloated. And grouchy." She holds out the electric kettle, which sags in her skinny arms. "I don't really need it."

Of course. Daddy sends her a menu of lead roles whenever she gets bored of the usual drugs.

The meanness of this thought catches me off guard, and I push it out of my head. Maybe the powder makes me grouchy, too. Orchid's been a good friend since sophomore year of undergrad: coming to all my performances, letting me bum a lot of those "usual drugs," charging barely anything to rent her extra room when I was struggling to find work after graduation.

Honestly, maybe Orchid just doesn't notice the weird god complex side effect because Orchid's got a permanent weird god complex. It's fine. It's not her fault for being raised by multimillionaires.

I focus on pouring the water over my herbal tea, then refresh my email for the zillionth time that day.

"So… if all the Victorian artists were eating mummies, how are there any left today? It's got to be a nonrenewable resource, right?"

She shrugs. "Probably they just found more. Or they buy them from the museums."

My jaw drops. "The museums would do that?"

"If they're paid well."

I frown into my tea, searching for the right words. "Does it bother you?"

"That it's expensive?"

"No." I know that expensive doesn't mean much to Orchid, whose producer dad can buy ancient bottles of wine at dinner on a whim. She didn't think twice about giving me the powder. "That it… it's history. Like, at one point that was a person. It'd be gross if someone ground you up and ate you, right?"

"They're dead." She stares at me. "Would you rather they just lie there? They're not even rotting." She takes her mug of coffee to the couch, then settles into a puddle of sunshine from the big window. "If you think about it, we're giving them the chance to live again, through the art. I wouldn't mind coming back as a song or a monologue."

I think about all the Victorian composers I know: Loder, McFarren, Barnett. I imagine Michael William Balfe blitzed off his mind, scribbling articulations above a tumult of chords. I could be convinced that *The Bohemian Girl* was written under the influence of mummy powder. I start to search online for if the Germans or Italians ever ate mummies—and my phone beeps.

It's the cast list. My breath catches as I open the email and scroll.

I don't have to scroll far. My name tops the list.

"Orchid. I did it."

"Hm?" She's lounging on the couch, thumbing through some influencer's feed.

"The lead. I'm Macbeth."

"Well, don't say it backstage," she says, forever superstitious. She turns back to her phone. "You're welcome."

"More energy, Jake," snaps the director, Stephan. "Try to come in on top of the note. Again."

Around me, the other singers arranged in a semicircle of black stacking chairs cross and uncross their legs, fidget with their sheet music. My costar Audrey gives me a stone-faced but encouraging nod. But behind her, Gordon is making an expression that suggests he'd rather understudy a screaming goat. It's been three weeks of rehearsal, and I've gone from being the director's pet to his ball and chain.

I've decided not to use the powder. Sure, my voice sounds like I'm channeling heaven's hottest angels, but the feeling during the auditions creeped me out, and the dreams afterwards just weren't worth it. I don't *like* feeling like Orchid, like some ancient king who expects sacrifices and submission.

Then again, how do I know how pharaohs thought or felt? Maybe they were chill, approachable celebrities, the Bill Murrays of ancient Egypt, and it's something else about the powder that gets me detached and condescending. It doesn't matter: I have the role, and I'll work my ass off until I deserve it.

Stephan pinches the air to conduct me in again, and I try miserably to echo the noise he's made.

"No." He waves away the accompanist, then demonstrates, repeating the passage I've just sung, eyebrows raised.

I hit the pitch with everything I've got. He shakes his head, but this time, he doesn't stop conducting. "Go over this one with your vocal coach," he calls, over the music, as Audrey's lush soprano fills the room.

I sink down in my chair. If things keep going this way, the Met won't be calling anytime soon.

—

The next week, Audrey motions me into the hallway after rehearsal, her dark eyes intense. Audrey is stoic but kind, and it's more than a little intimidating to be cast alongside someone with so much more professional experience. I'm barely out of undergrad; most professionals at the Carolan have their doctorate in vocal performance.

"What's up?" I ask.

She walks me down the hall, farther out of earshot, and my throat tightens with every step of our feet on the tile.

When she finally stops and turns to me, her voice is low and urgent. "Stephan asked me how I felt about my stage chemistry with Gordon."

It's like a punch to the diaphragm. Outside of rehearsal, I've been practicing more than I ever have—but I'm apparently mediocre enough to consider replacing me with the understudy just a few weeks into the production. I picture the jar of awful black powder, sitting untouched in my makeup kit. My stomach churns.

I steady myself. "What did you tell him?"

"I told him Gordon and I don't see eye to eye, but I'd be professional if I had to work with him." She presses her lips together. "Instead of saying that Gordon's a social-climbing bastard who'd fry and eat a baby if it got him more solo time. Could you please get your shit together?"

Her eyes nail me to the wall.

"I mean, yeah." I shuffle my feet. "Does Stephan know you're telling me this?"

"Stephan doesn't care who's in the lead as long as the show doesn't flop."

I wince. "Sorry. Thanks for the heads-up." Audrey is still staring at me, so I add: "I guess I haven't been practicing as much. I just have to buckle down again."

Her eyebrows knit together. "You're better than that," she scolds. "Don't be one of those artists who gets lazy once they've got a lead."

She turns on her heel, and I stand in the hallway for a long time.

I could let them demote me to where I deserve to be. I could audition when I'm better, stronger, more developed. I could let this opportunity pass me by and hope that I get another someday.

The thought makes me nauseous.

———

Before rehearsal the next day, I mix a pinch of powdered mummy into an opaque water bottle. I probably don't need as much as I took for the first auditions. As we shuffle the chairs into position, I take a swig and hold it under my tongue. The taste of watered-down jerky lingers on my breath, and there's a pit of dread in my stomach. *That was a person. I've just eaten some bit of a person.*

An unwelcome image flits across my mind: some twerp biting off a hunk of Audrey's flesh, chewing, swallowing. I nearly throw up.

But when the powder kicks in, the sound of my own voice is a hot knife, cutting down all my doubts.

"*There* it is!" Stephan beams, and Gordon rolls his eyes, and Audrey shoots me a relieved micro-nod. I feel radiant. I want to soak this feeling in a sponge and bathe in it every morning. It's obvious now that this powder is from an ancient god-king; it's the only way to explain why my voice sounds like it's sparkling down from the sun itself.

When I reach to turn the page, my hand brushes the music stand—and I flinch at the sudden pang of heat. It feels like a pan fresh out of the oven.

I sip the laced water strategically for the rest of the rehearsal, and the mood of the whole cast is lighter. Why was I so worried? Orchid was right. Pharaoh or not, if that mummy could hear what they were being sublimated into, they'd probably applaud too.

After rehearsal, as I organize my sheet music back into my binder, Stephan claps me on the shoulder.

"Auditions for *Don Giovanni* are in a few weeks," he says. "Whatever you've been doing, keep it up."

I smile back. Maybe I'd play Don Giovanni in the next production. Or maybe I'd look into more prestigious opera houses. For the first time, I realize, I'm dreaming of more than chorus roles and making rent.

With the talent this powder unlocks, I could be the best of all time.

———

I am onstage, facing a theater stuffed with bodies. Each breath lifts my feet off the ground a little higher, like I'm inhaling helium instead of oxygen. The audience gasps when they realize I'm floating. Audrey is beside me, shouting, grabbing first at my waist and then my legs, nagging me to come down. But she's not part of the sky; she doesn't know how the music is supposed to go, and so I kick her in the stomach, and she lets go, and the art is perfect.

———

Orchid stretches her legs across the fire escape stairs and coughs out a puff of smoke. "So has anything bad happened yet?"

My heart stops. "What?"

It's Wednesday of tech week, and I've taken my dusty communion every day at rehearsal. A lot of bad things *have* happened—and then I wake up, feeling guilty that

I don't feel guilty. Right now, I'm avoiding sleeping by smoking on the fire escape with Orchid.

My voice is so strong that I don't even need to worry about what the smoke or lack of sleep will do to it. The effects seem to last longer and longer the more I use. It's as if each swallow of the powder lingers in my body, the mummy's atoms mixing with my own, and it needs only a taste to remember the inhuman abilities. I can feel the effects of tonight's powder as if I'd taken it seconds ago, but Orchid's question shakes me even through the confidence high.

Orchid raises her eyebrows at me. "You're doing *the Scottish play?*"

I relax: just Orchid being woo-woo.

"So far so good." I inhale, hold the tobacco on my tongue, drawing out the moment of relief as the cigarette smoke supersedes the powder's flavor. Then I exhale, and the aftertaste of salt and embalming fluids floods back into my mouth. "They're a little behind in building the catwalk."

"The catwalk? Doesn't that come with the theater?"

"Not the one for lights. This one's part of the set, like, an elevated platform for the second floor of the castle. The witches start the show on it, and Audrey does the whole sleepwalking aria from up there, and some of our duets—"

"Cool." Orchid says distantly, rubbing her arms in the night air and looking thoughtfully at the window. She stubs out her cigarette and stands. "Hey, it's cold. I'm going in."

I shift to let her step around me, annoyed at her abruptness, and faintly confused at my own irritation. Orchid's brusque manners never bothered me before.

I should probably be more concerned at this emerging part of me that expects attention, worship, power. Maybe I've gotten used to people stopping their work to hang enraptured on my every syllable. Or maybe consuming ancient history makes it obvious how ephemeral and insignificant the average person is. Almost everyone's just a body, waiting to decay.

I shiver, looking out at the headlights marching through the night like an army of fireflies. And then, as if for the first time, I notice the metal rails between me and the city below, and another shiver sends excitement pumping through my veins.

How much power do I really have? How much control?

I scoot closer to the rails, leaning in, focusing on the metal—and breathe, deep and rhythmic, tasting on every exhale the things inside me that were never allowed to rot.

When I reach my hands out, slowly, a searing heat radiates from the rails.

I smile, looking down at the city below, at the cars and streetlights and telephone wires and all the possibilities for my life. I could make history.

—

It's funny, I think, as I tap a little extra powder into my water on opening night. A long time ago, someone worked so hard to dry this body out, to preserve it forever. It only takes me a moment to wet it down and swallow it.

My entry onstage is incandescent. Deafening applause follows my duet with Banquo, and I wonder what the *Times* critic will publish tomorrow. I have no doubt that I'm impressing the right people, that I'll be at the big professional houses soon. I'll make enough money to move out of Orchid's extra room, to buy the powder straight from Orchid's dealer. I'm not sure how much more powder I'll even need; the changes wrought by that small spice jar aren't fading. Maybe they're permanent.

And so, I stand in the wings, watching Audrey sing her first aria, waving around a letter that describes the witches' prophecies.

I can't believe I didn't notice before. She's doing it wrong.

"*Che tardi? Accetta il dono, ascendivi a regnar...*"

Her vibrato is rich, but it's new-money rich. There's something missing from her performed ambition. It grates on me through the rest of her solo, through our duet planning the murder, through the choral number mourning the King.

I carry the dummy prop of Duncan's corpse offstage and wonder idly: how much god was in a Western king? And our modern rulers: the CEOs and billionaires and celebrities of the world. Would the worship of headlines and business reports and Instagram captions turn them into gods? Could they apotheosize by holding history under their tongue?

When the curtain drops, I pull Audrey into my dressing room.

"Are you okay?" she asks, looking concerned. "You look upset. You've been doing great."

"I realized something during your first aria."

"What?"

"You just… don't seem truly ambitious. I don't feel it under my skin the way I should."

Her face goes wooden. "Let's let Stephan handle notes after the show, shall we?"

She turns to leave, but I catch her arm. I'd thought that greatness was a mountain I'd have to climb alone, but why should I have to?

"I've got something that can help right now. We could both wow the critics tonight."

"You're being an asshole." She says it with no rancor, just bluntly.

"I'm being extremely generous," I assure her, and I offer her my water bottle.

She stares at it.

"Thank you," she deadpans. "I've been tossing and turning over my utility bill."

"It's not about the water." I roll my eyes, grab a clear plastic cup from the dressing room table, and pour a tiny sip into it. Audrey's already quite talented; she won't need much.

She takes the cup and peers at it, wrinkles her nose at the particles swirling in the cup. "Why's it got crap in it?"

"It's a drug my roommate gave me." I lower my voice. "It's mummy. Dried pharaoh powder."

A laugh bursts out of her. "Number one, that's not possible. Number two, gross."

"The Victorians used to do it," I insist.

"Yeah, I saw that Smithsonian article too, but come on—"

"Orchid says it connects her to the muses."

"Okay, problematic, did no one *ever* make you read Edward Said—"

"You've heard the difference."

She freezes, her eyes flitting between me and the water, a lovely shadow of doubt in her dark eyes. Her throat works as she composes herself.

"You're saying you really believe that's the ground-up body of an ancient dead guy."

"The ancient dead guy isn't using the body," I reassure her. "He's not even rotting."

I hold out the water again, and she takes the plastic cup in shaky hands, frowning at it.

"I can't wait to see how you sound," I tell her.

"You think this was a person."

I nod. "Not just any person. A part of history. Like we could be."

When Audrey speaks next, her voice is soft and gentle, watching the powder dancing in the water as if she's speaking to the man inside. Her eyes are fiery, flickering up to mine.

"And you'd still swallow them?"

I press my lips into a line.

She doesn't break eye contact as she bangs the cup pointedly down on the dressing room table—right onto a precarious pile of sheet music. The papers slip, slow-motion like a landslide, and the cup succumbs to the undertow, too fast for Audrey to catch it. The liquid inside dribbles out onto the papers, a waste and a blasphemy, and Audrey tenses, an unreadable expression on her face, before shaking her head and bolting from the dressing room.

A cold certainty dawns on me as the door slams behind her. Audrey will not be joining me on my ascent to greatness.

—

She ignores me in the wings during Acts II and III, shuts herself in her dressing room during the next intermissions. But she can't hide forever. I wait backstage as the lights go up on her final appearance in Act IV.

"*Una macchia è qui tuttora…*"

Audrey's bare feet stagger dramatically onto the catwalk for her most famous aria. She stumbles, mimicking a sleepwalker's unsteadiness. The audience is rapt; the Doctor and the Lady who eavesdrop on Lady Macbeth's dazed confession hit their marks under the catwalk.

I take a sip from my bottle. When I'm done here, they'll blame the curse. They'll think that Audrey has truly gone mad. But she won't be able to sleepwalk for a long time.

Even in the stage lights, I can see the soles of her feet turning pink where they hit the metal catwalk. I take another sip, keep my focus as I feel the power surging through my veins.

Audrey is moving too quickly for the song now, rocking back and forth on her toes. The eavesdroppers in the scene frown up at her; they can only feel the usual warmth from standing in the lights in costume. Someone behind me mutters something about pitchiness.

There's no way down for Audrey except the stairs offstage, and by the time she glances towards the wings, it's too late. The panic in her voice is real now; there's no way for her to understand what's happening. The Doctor and the Lady exchange confused glances, likely wondering why she hasn't fallen to her knees to cry about the invisible blood on her hands.

Instead of falling in supplication, Audrey reaches for the metal handrails of the platform—and finds relief. I haven't been heating these. Ever the professional, she sublimates her fear and relief into her performance, staring with wide eyes at the white knuckles gripping the rails for balance. She lifts herself onto them, a respite from the burning of her feet. The rails rattle with each breath, but they hold her weight.

It's really a shame. Her understudy won't be able to recreate this kind of performance. But her sacrilege can't go unpunished.

She's nearing the end of the aria, and I imagine she plans to sprint offstage and soothe her burned feet in cool water. She'll wonder if the stage lights were too hot, too close to the catwalk.

I focus all of my energy on the joints of the handrails.

Audrey holds her final note; the Lady and the Doctor close out the aria by praying for mercy from a god that Audrey has disgraced. The lights go down; a scrim descends that will mask the catwalk for my next scene.

The audience's applause masks the crash of the handrail as it hits the stage floor, fifteen feet below.

And I step from the wings back into the light.

———

"… a concussion, several broken ribs, and her feet got some sort of friction burn on the way down. She's pretty banged up, but she'll be okay in a few months."

Stephan leans against the door of the green room, reading us the text updates from the assistant stage manager who accompanied Audrey to the ER. There's a murmur of relief from the rest of the cast, crowded together on the faded couches. I dab my face with a makeup remover wipe I borrowed from someone's bag. I just want to go home.

"Now, I know a lot is going to be said about the curse," Stephan sighs.

My throat clenches. Why did Audrey have to act out tonight? Now all the headlines will be about the accident.

"For your own peace of mind," he continues, "we'll be reviewing the whole set design to make sure everything is safe. That said, please, *please* don't use props or set pieces in ways we haven't rehearsed. Tonight is a great example of why we don't spontaneously change blocking onstage."

Despite my irritation, I can't keep the corners of my lips still. Stephan pauses, his gaze lingering on me a moment too long.

He follows me to my dressing room after the rest of his announcements (Pamela will be taking over the role of Lady MacBeth, he'll keep us posted about Audrey, aside from all that great job tonight).

"You okay?" He shuts the door behind us, eyebrows knit in concern.

"Yeah," I shrug, zipping my eyeliner into my makeup bag. And I mean it. Why lie to him? I'm the breakout star that will make his name, the gravity drawing audiences to the ticket booth.

"You worked closer with her than anyone else," he probes.

"I think maybe it was fate that she fell. A god's will."

He studies me then, a strange, hard look. I return his gaze, steady and impassive and room-temperature.

Finally, he looks away, swallows hard. "Well, I guess let's pray that there aren't any more incidents in this run."

I make no promises.

As he slips out the door, he gives me one last nod. "You sounded great tonight. I bet we get some stellar reviews."

——

I'm in a desert of blue skies and warm sands. I hum a tune, and the desert hums with me. When I glance behind me, someone is crawling across the dunes towards me, but I can't hear what she's wailing. It doesn't matter.

At my feet, the supplicant is drying out, shrinking as I tap my feet in time with my song. Her eyes recede, lips pulling back until the white of her teeth gleams bright against the darkening skin. Broken bones rise up against her tightening skin like a breaching shark.

When the song is over, I snap off a limb and bite. Above me, the clouds are fluffy white. I'll draw straight lines in the sand.

I taste like death, but I sound divine. And soon, I shall be king.

THE TELLTALE LVAD

MEG CANDELARIA

"This is creepy," Eva—Dr. Eva Hernandez, MD, PhD to you—said, as she began infusing formaldehyde, desiccant, DMSO, and other chemicals she would rather not think too much about through the IV that had been placed in the body before it was a dead body, that is, when it, or rather he, had been a critically-ill patient. Her words were muffled and her movements made slightly clumsy by her biohazard suit, but she would not have removed it for anything at this moment.

"It's beyond creepy," Laura—Doctor, but, despite her best efforts, not Professor, Laura Eisloffel, PhD—said, while injecting a pink fluid into a port connected to the body's cranial cavity and withdrawing cerebrospinal fluid from the same port.

"So why are we doing this?" Hernandez asked.

Eisloffel shrugged, but did not look up from her efforts. The fluid was thick and difficult to inject, not to mention dangerous.

"He's leaving us basically his entire estate on the condition that we mummify his body and send it to the museum as a replica mummy. So, I suppose we could say it's for the money? Or out of respect for our employer's wishes? Or to give the museum a mummy it can display without controversy or guilt?"

"Right," Hernandez sighed. She contemplated the blood draining out of the IV on the opposite side of the body. After a moment she said, "We're sure he's dead, right? I don't want to accidentally murder my employer, even if he is a billionaire."

"He's dead," Eisloffel said with certainty. "As you know better than I do, Dr. Hernandez, MD."

"Imagine if we're wrong, though," Hernandez said, looking at the body uncomfortably. "I keep thinking about how he would get that look on his face right before he screamed at someone and then fired them for not doing his bidding exactly as he required."

"The key word here is 'dead.' He can't scream at us or fire us."

Hernandez nodded. "I know, I know. Maybe I'm just psyching myself out. His EEG showed no activity. He doesn't breathe on his own. No reaction to any stimulus. No spontaneous movement. Definitely dead. I guess it's the ventricular assist device still pumping that makes it seem so eerie. Especially since it doesn't produce any pulse, even when the person is alive. It makes me want to double check everything."

Eisloffel glanced up as she refilled her syringe. She paused and listened for a moment. "It's definitely eerie. It doesn't sound like a heartbeat."

"Left ventricular assist devices (LVADs) don't squeeze and relax like the heart does, they just sort of push continuously," Hernandez said with a slight smile. "I'm going into 'lecture the patient' mode, aren't I? Anyway, it doesn't sound like a normal heartbeat, but it does sound like a functioning heart once you get used to it."

"Well, in any case, we can turn that off when you're done."

Hernandez looked at the fluid draining from the body. It was now the same clear, slightly green tinge of the fluid being infused in. "I'm done with the infusion now," she said. "And the drainage from the desiccation won't need pumping."

She turned to the bank of equipment by the bed, found the correct instrument, and pushed the button to power down the artificial heart. The sudden absence of the sound was startling.

Eisloffel continued her work.

Hernandez watched fluid drain from the body contemplatively.

"How did the ancient Egyptians do this anyway?" she asked. "It's not like they had IVs and all this—" She waved her hand at the scores of equipment in the room.

"They took out most of the organs and stuffed the body with something or another, I think," Eisloffel replied. "The climate took care of the rest."

After some time, Eisloffel finished adding the preserving solution to the brain. She put down her syringe, straightened, and stretched. "How's the desiccation going?"

"Looks good. The body's pretty dried. Apart from that shit you're putting in around the brain. How is suspending the brain in glucose-containing liquid not going to cause mold, bacteria, and other gunk to grow?"

"Nothing grows in the preserving solution. We've tried to culture bacteria, fungi, and even protozoa in it, they just don't grow. The solution just preserves the brain in a sort of suspended state, keeping it from rotting or getting infected, which isn't really proper for a mummy that's supposed to simulate an ancient Egyptian mummy, but the boss wanted it for some reason. Maybe he couldn't stand the thought of his big, beautiful brain being destroyed."

Hernandez snorted, "Big, beautiful brain, my ass. He never did anything but provide funding, terrorize newbies, and get in the way."

The two removed the remaining medical equipment from the body.

"Time to wrap him up," Eisloffel said. "Can you put the diagram up, just to verify?"

Hernandez looked at her hands. "I should change my gloves before I handle the computer," she said, looking uneasily at the stains on her gloves.

"Don't take off your gloves!" Eisloffel snapped. "This shit is toxic and it'll go right through the skin. Just open the computer. Everything in this room is going to get thoroughly decontaminated and most of it burned anyway."

"Right," Hernandez said, flipping on a screen.

An image of a mummy appeared, with a detailed breakdown of how the wrappings were placed around the body. They both studied the page for a few moments then began bandaging the body as shown, starting with wrapping the arms. As they lifted the body's arms to wrap them, they heard a sudden "whoosh" from the body.

"Shit!" Eisloffel yelled.

Hernandez jumped and backed away as far as she could.

The LVAD had restarted.

"Well, that was disturbing," Hernandez said, stepping back towards the body. "I'd forgotten that he had one of those high-tech vent assist devices that restarts when the body moves. It must have kicked back on when we moved the body. It's supposed to be a fail-safe against it being turned off from the outside while someone is still alive. Not sure how well it works."

"Good for scaring the crap out of people though," Eisloffel agreed, slightly embarrassed at her initial reaction.

"Yeah, I was about to think… well, just for one moment."

"We should warn the museum people."

"Definitely. We wouldn't want them to think the mummy is cursed."

They returned to wrapping the body, ignoring the continued sounds from the LVAD.

When the body matched the image on the screen, they sprayed the mummy with a sealant that would ensure none of the fluids inside the mummy would leak out and endanger the museum personnel.

After a last double-check to ensure all was well, the two women stepped into an antechamber that had been made into a makeshift decontamination room. They rid themselves of their suits and performed the necessary cleaning procedures.

"I'm glad we don't have to clean up the room and do the actual delivery," Hernandez murmured.

"Agreed," Eisloffel said. "And now that we've fulfilled our obligation to our donor, we can get back to work. How's that siRNA project you were telling me about going?"

"Erg. RNA is so difficult. It falls apart if you look at it the wrong way. But I think I've found a way to stabilize it without affecting the function."

They left the hospital chatting about future work, the mummy all but forgotten.

—

The billionaire returned to consciousness slowly. He attempted to move and found that he could not. Although he had expected this and had no great fear of enclosed places, the paralysis would have induced panic in him while he was alive. Now, however, with mood stabilizing chemicals in place of adrenalin and other panic-inducing hormones flooding his brain, he simply waited patiently.

By the time he was moved to his new home in the anthropology department of the museum, he was able to make slight movements. He wiggled his fingers.

"Did you see that?" an alarmed voice asked.

"See what?" another voice answered.

"I could have sworn I saw the mummy's fingers move. Just a little."

"Late night last night?"

"I'm not drunk or hungover."

"Just a trick of the light."

"Yeah, must have been."

"The noise from the undead cyber heart isn't helping."

"Yeah, but the heart's going because we moved the body. The docs said this would happen."

The billionaire felt himself being lifted and put into a sarcophagus. The door to the case was left partially open to allow visitors to view both the mummy and the decorated sarcophagus.

After a time, the billionaire heard a door close and then silence. He could, of course, see nothing. He regretted the loss of sight, but sacrifices must be made. He would be compensated for the loss soon enough. He waited. All was quiet except for an odd rushing sound that felt familiar but that he could not quite place.

Movement continued to return. Soon he was able to move all of his limbs, albeit with considerable limitations due to the bandages. Eventually, he decided it was time to test the situation further. He slowly put his arms out and pushed the mummy case open further, far enough to allow him to walk slowly and carefully out of it. The display case took a bit more time, but only a bit. Soon he was feeling his way through the Hall of Ancient Peoples.

He heard footsteps coming nearer. Heavy, slow footsteps. A guard, perhaps. The billionaire moved to what he hoped was a dark corner and waited, hands outstretched. All was still except for the annoying rushing sound. Where had he heard that before? He put it out of his mind as unimportant for now.

He waited until the footsteps stopped and the person screamed. Hidden behind the mummy's wrappings, the billionaire smiled. This moment, the moment of terror before the inevitable acquiescence, had always been his favorite part of any scheme. The mummy had only a few seconds to act, but that was enough. He reached out and touched the screaming man. Immediately, the man fell silent.

The billionaire smirked beneath his bandages. The scientists he had hired to help him were fools, he thought. They had not realized the true nature of the solution they had infused into his body. It was not a mere preservative, but something more. A solution that, along with his natural charisma, would enthrall any person he touched. Nor had they realized the weakness of the coating meant to keep the preserving solution inside the mummy. The coating was malleable, controllable. The solution would leak only when and where he wanted it to. And of course, he had cleverly ensured that different teams worked on each component, so that none of them would realize what they had made.

His speech was distorted by the bandages and inaudible when he first spoke. He remembered that he must breathe during speech. His second attempt went better. "You are mine," he told the guard. "You will do as I say."

"Of course," the guard replied.

"Bring others to me," the billionaire said. "One at a time for now."

"Who?"

"Everyone eventually. For now, your coworkers. The museum will be mine."

"Yes."

"Carry on as usual otherwise. Don't attract suspicion."

"Yes."

"You may go now. Complete your rounds."

The guard walked off.

My first slave, the billionaire thought. He savored the moment, his enjoyment marred only slightly by the continued background sound. He recognized it now: it was the sound of the device that had kept his heart going for as long as it had. He had insisted that the best possible, most updated version be implanted. It had worked all too well, it seemed.

The mummy contemplated his next move. He could not count on the guard to bring him everyone he needed. He would walk further afield. To the back rooms where the curators worked. To the streets. He need have little fear of getting caught prematurely: if he simply slumped to the ground, it would be assumed that the mummy was moved as a prank. After all, what fool would believe in a walking mummy in this day and age? But even this deceit was only a temporary need. Eventually, no one would wonder or be able to wonder.

He smiled as best he could under the bandages. Money was a wonderful tool, but it was, in the end, not sufficient. Too many rivals. Too many restrictions. Too much need to pretend to care and follow the laws. As a mummy, he didn't need to fill out tax forms or lobby the government. He only needed to conquer.

But that would have to wait for now. He must move slowly, enthralling only a few people at first, to avoid premature suspicions. For now, he must make his way back to the case and stay there through the day. Until night arrived again and brought more lone people to make his own.

He had an excellent sense of direction and walked back to the display case confidently, only to find that it was not the right one. The museum was ridiculously complicated. No one could have found the right display the first time. He frowned slightly, restricted still by the bandages. Why did he not insist on becoming a Peruvian mummy, he wondered. The bandages were a tactical error, a limitation. He pawed at the bandages, shifting them until he could open one eye. He could see the display case containing the mummy case and other artifacts clearly now, directly across the room from where he stood. He paused to consider how badly the museum's designers had failed in its layout to allow this to happen.

The sound of his heart, whooshing in an attempt to move blood that wasn't there, was an annoyance as well. Why couldn't it beat like a normal heart? A slow, inexorable heartbeat coming closer and closer would add to his victim's fear as he stalked them and make his conquest that much more enjoyable. But this whooshing sound was not in the least bit scary! It would just be in the way and make stealth more difficult.

Well, no matter. He would prevail. He always prevailed.

He finally found the right case crawled inside, and waited for his chance to make the world anew.

SERVANTS OF FROST AND MADNESS

ZACH SHEPHARD

The dark spot on the ice stood out like a melanoma, marring Greenland's corpse-pale skin. Amy couldn't help but laugh; it was probably nothing, but of course she saw the blemish as a symptom of disease. After all, the team was there to study the Earth's health. Seemed fitting she'd find signs of cancer.

She stopped her snowmobile a safe distance away and raised a hand against the arctic sun. The dark object jutted from the snow like a tiny teepee, ankle high, its canvas stretched too tight over its frame. The color reminded Amy of burnt sugar: a little black, a little orange, all mottled. Maybe *this* was something

Dr. Malam would finally let her write an honest report about. It'd be a welcome change from having her research corrupted or ignored.

Amy approached the thing in the ice. She only made it three steps before the pain struck.

It shot through her head like an icicle arrow, in one temple and out the other. Sharp, cold, sudden—and gone as quickly as it had arrived. All that remained was a spiky chill behind her eyes, like creeping frost filling her neural pathways.

Amy shook the sensation away. She'd clearly been out exploring too long. No one else had ventured this far from camp, and maybe this was why. Too much time in the cold. She resolved to make her investigation a quick one.

Amy knelt by the object. She'd figured it for a rock, but the texture was off—and why would one be out here anyway? She unfolded a knife and carefully dug around the base. More and more of that same burnt-sugar color was exposed, until Amy finally realized what she was looking at.

An elbow.

An elbow, pointed at the sky, mummified by the cold. Any muscle beneath the skin had long since withered away.

Awe and wonder gave Amy pause, but something in that frost behind her eyes told her to keep digging. So she did.

Snow whisked away; more leathery flesh emerged. The sun continued its descent into the white horizon.

Evening on the ice sheet only lasted a few hours at that time of year, but it was dark and cold enough for Amy to accept she couldn't finish the excavation now. She fought off the compulsion to continue digging and mounted her snowmobile.

Casting one last glance over her shoulder, she saw the grotesque angles of the exposed limbs, protruding from Greenland's icy body like needles from a voodoo doll. Among the disturbed powder lay the face of the deceased, turned toward Amy, staring with those skin-sealed eye sockets. The man—yes, it was a man, Amy somehow knew—had no nose, no upper lip. As Amy drove away, she saw in her mind's eye that set of clenched, yellow-brown teeth.

They looked angry.

———

The main dome's interior resembled a workshop: plywood walls, metal supports, lots of open area. Small tables with cheap plastic folding chairs littered the place. Amy found Dr. Malam at the kitchen stove, alone. The square-jawed, thick-knuckled man glanced up from the frying pan he tended.

"It's late," Dr. Malam said, resuming his stirring. "You should be in your yurt."

"I found something outside. Something big."

"Leave your data on the table. I'll review it as I eat."

"No—it's not about that. It's a body."

"A body?"

"An old one. Mummified." Amy struggled to articulate her thoughts, like her tongue was wrapped in a tight leather sheath. "It feels… off."

Dr. Malam gave her a look—the same one he gave all his researchers when he was about to dismiss their ideas.

"You should get some rest. We can talk about your 'mummy' tomorrow."

"This is serious. Whatever's out there isn't right. It's—"

Punish.

Amy's brows furrowed. "What?"

"What do you mean, 'what?'"

"Why am I getting punished?"

"You're not. Although maybe you will be, if you don't let me eat in peace. Go to bed, Amy."

In a stupor, Amy turned away. Her legs carried her through bewilderment's fog and out of the dome. She stopped on the snow, gazing in the direction of the mummy. Somewhere in the low light, it lay like shrapnel jutting from the world's icy flesh. Amy wanted to go back. She wanted to keep digging. But the wind was picking up, sending wispy waves across the sea of snow. Tomorrow. Tomorrow, she'd finish digging the thing up. And Dr. Malam would have no choice but to acknowledge what she'd found.

Amy trudged to her yurt. She shut off the light and lay on the bunk, staring at the darkened ceiling.

The wind howled sharper than usual.

———

Amy splashed water from the basin onto her face. She wiped it away and looked in the mirror.

She laughed.

It was silly, thinking about how worked up she'd gotten the previous day. Dr. Malam had been dismissive of her, sure—but that's just how he was. Things would change once Amy showed him the mummy. He wouldn't be able to sweep a corpse under the rug as easily as he did her other findings.

They met in the main dome, at one of the small breakfast tables. The other researchers had already finished up and shuffled off to work.

"Think of what this means," Amy said, buttering her toast. "A mummy exposed by melting ice. Clear evidence of climate change. And this is something that'll interest the average person a lot more than some graphs they don't understand."

Dr. Malam chewed a long while, eyes on his meal.

"We're climatologists," he finally said, "not anthropologists. Whatever you found out there is beyond the scope of our report."

"Seriously? This is a big deal. And it absolutely belongs in our report."

Dr. Malam pointed his fork at Amy. "You may still be in grad school, but this is real-world stuff you're working on. When you're part of a research team, you follow directions. Sooner you learn that, the better."

"So what's our report supposed to say? 'Everything's good, but it'd be even better if we burned more fossil fuels'?"

"We're not having this discussion again."

Of course they weren't. Amy wasn't even there to do real research; she was there for the optics of her name on the report. After all, if even an enthusiastic grad student believed climate change was no real concern, surely there was nothing to worry about. Senator Jenkins and his Big-Oil buddies just needed approval from the younger generation. And Dr. Malam just needed those extra digits in his bank account.

"All right," Dr. Malam said, wiping a napkin across his mouth. "Let's have a look at this mummy."

He insisted on driving the snowmobile, even though Amy was the one navigating. The previous night's winds had blown snow across her trail like makeup covering a scar, but she knew just the patch of ice to look for.

It was empty.

Amy leapt off the stopped snowmobile. She ran to where the mummy had been.

"I don't understand," she said. "It was right here." She dropped to her hands and knees, shoveling big handfuls of snow to either side. A clump of it struck Dr. Malam's leg as he arrived. His sigh was as cold as a Greenland wind.

"You need a break," he said. "There's a supply plane coming in tomorrow. Take it back to town when it leaves. Stay there a while. You can return when you're feeling better."

Dr. Malam drew Amy to her feet; in her confusion, she didn't resist. They mounted the snowmobile. As they drove off, Amy looked back at the snow she'd dug through. Just beside the disturbed mess was a strange mark.

She didn't remember making that handprint.

———

Amy was halfway through packing for her trip when she decided she needed advice. Johnny wasn't in the dome's kitchen, which meant she'd find him in the freezer.

The path to her destination was a trench cut ten feet deep into the snow. It ended in a man-made cave filled with shelves of perishable foods. Chef Johnny rummaged through the boxes, cursing to himself. He didn't stop digging when he noticed Amy.

"Fucking *rats*, man."

Amy glanced around. "Rats?"

"Last job I had was on a ship. Always had rats gettin' their bitch-ass teeth into the food. That's why I signed up for this arctic bullshit. Figured no rat could survive up here. But they followed me along anyway."

Amy let out a small laugh. Johnny's unfiltered thoughts always cheered her up.

"We don't have rats, Johnny."

"Then I guess we've got a fuckin' *polar bear* problem, because something got into the sausages." He slid a cardboard box halfway off the shelf for Amy to see. The corner had been torn open.

"Maybe Doc just really wanted some reindeer."

"We all want reindeer—shit's delicious. But most of us got the decency to open a box like a normal human being. Hey—you seen my favorite knife anywhere?"

"You have a favorite knife?"

"'Course I got a favorite knife. The one with the whale-bone handle. Real nice. Couldn't find it this morning."

"I'm sure it'll turn up."

"It'd better. We only got twenty people up here. If some motherfucker stole my knife, I'll find him. Masterson thought maybe it was down here—like I'd use my best knife to slice open boxes." He cursed and resumed searching.

"Can't hurt to look, I guess. Hey—can I ask you something?"

"Do it."

"Dr. Malam wants to send me into town for a while. He thinks the cold is getting to me. Or the isolation. Or—I don't know. I think he just wants to get rid of me."

Johnny lost control of a box. It fell to the snow, vegetables toppling out. He dropped an f-bomb that filled the cave. He crouched to clean up.

"Anyway, I was wondering—do you think I should go? Or should I push back on this?"

Escape.

"Yeah," Amy said. "Not a bad idea, I guess."

Johnny looked up. "Huh?"

"Escaping. Getting out of here for a while."

"Oh—hell yes. We could all use a vacation from that asshole." Johnny put the box back on the shelf. "Sounds like you've got your answer. Don't know what you need me for."

"Thanks, Johnny. I've gotta go pack. Good luck with the knife."

"Whalebone handle," he said. "You see it, you send it my way. Cool?"

"Cool."

"Have fun, Ames. And bring me back some rat poison."

Amy returned to her yurt and resumed packing. As she drifted off to sleep that night, a familiar chill crawled its way into her brain.

———

She stood on an ice sheet she knew well, but this wasn't Greenland. This was a time before nations.

Amy felt no familiar cold, no lacerating wind. Instead she experienced weightlessness as she flowed across the snow, leaving no prints in her wake. The world gleamed with a pearly coating like clamshell nacre. Land and sky merged as one.

A dozen figures in thick furs gathered on the barren snow. Just as a ghost observes the living, Amy watched their story unfold from afar.

A man stepped forth, dropped to his knees. He drew curved designs in the ice with a crude knife. In the twisted logic of dreams, Amy found she knew things about him: he was a holy man; a sorcerer. Like all others in that place, he feared the great god Pahnukh. And it was because of this fear that he'd suggested the ritual—the only way to appease the God of Frost and Madness.

The sorcerer finished his ice-carving and set his blade aside. The tribe's chief, bearing seal-tooth jewelry, handed him a piece of dried reindeer meat.

The sorcerer placed the meat on his tongue. He closed his eyes. The chief picked up the knife, uttered a short prayer to Pahnukh, and opened the willing sorcerer's throat.

He fell forward, blood running into the design's grooves like the flow of icy streams. Every slender curve filled to the brim, stark red against the white. The design flared brightly. The world changed.

Amy's eyes recovered from the flash to find a crimson hellscape. The ice had become muscle—living muscle, bright red, swelling and contracting in sync with the very Earth's respiration. The sky's color had changed to match, dotted with blood-cell clouds.

Behind the tribe stood a figure, thrice the tallest man's height. Its reindeer skull lay atop hulking, hunched shoulders as rocky as coastal cliffs. Overly long arms extended to the ground and ended in tree-root fingers. The loinclothed figure was painted red in the eerie light, but gave off the white sparkle of sunstruck ice.

Towering Pahnukh reached out a wooden hand, palm upturned. The chief placed in it the whalebone knife used in the sacrifice. Everyone dropped to their knees and bowed to the God of Frost and Madness.

A gurgling growl rang through the red air. For the first time in that place, the ghost of Amy felt a chill.

The sorcerer, dead on his bloody design, pointed a trembling arm at her. His wet, guttural call shook the world.

Everyone rose from their prostrations. They fixed on Amy. Pahnukh himself turned his reindeer-skull gaze on her.

The god advanced.

One heavy step after another, Pahnukh's hooves struck the meaty earth. Amy turned and ran. The stomping chased her, slow but consistent. She risked a glance backwards. Pahnukh, nearly upon her, reached out one sprawling hand, a small whalebone knife lodged in its wood.

Amy fell. Into a chasm she tumbled, sinking through sudden darkness. She screamed as the antlered god above peered over the edge, growing ever distant.

She shot up in bed.

Darkness surrounded, but she recognized her location: the yurt. Everything was normal. She brought her hands to her face, tried to control her breathing. Sweat soaked her clothes and hair. She heard faint echoes of the pursuing footsteps in her head.

No—it wasn't in her head. It came from outside. Something was crunching through the snow.

The footsteps circled the yurt. They stopped. Something outside prodded the canvas, rattling the yurt's lattice-frame wall. The steps resumed, stopped again. The structure shook once more. It continued in this way, like an animal searching for weakness in a fence. Amy followed the sounds with her eyes, through the darkness. They neared the door across the yurt.

She scooted backwards in bed, against the wall, pulling the blanket up to her chin. She didn't know what to do. There was no rational thought—only panic.

The door rattled. The entire yurt shook. A sudden wind howled. Amy grabbed a flashlight and aimed it at the door. She clicked it on.

The rattling stopped. Everything went quiet. Somewhere in the cold dark of Amy's mind, she felt the faintest sensation of an unspoken message, receding into the distance.

Sacrifice... spoiled.

With a trembling hand she placed the flashlight on the floor, its beam aimed at the yurt's door throughout the night.

The plane couldn't take off quickly enough. Amy had boarded right away instead of helping the crew unload supplies. She sat alone, wincing every time she heard a thud from the cargo area. When it was all done she saw the crew head to the main dome for their usual coffee with the researchers. As she waited, the previous night's experience ran through her mind like a movie she couldn't turn off. She could still hear the crunching footsteps of whatever had visited her yurt, as if they were just outside the plane.

The crew took an eternity to return. When the plane finally climbed into the sky, Amy felt an enormous weight lifted from her shoulders.

At Nuuk Airport, a thought struck: she didn't ever want to go back. The break Dr. Malam had suggested wouldn't change what might be waiting for her at camp. She couldn't stomach the idea of another night alone in that yurt, on the same frozen plain that had turned to living flesh in her dream.

But there was still the issue of the report. Amy had a chance to make things better—to show everyone the damage they were doing to the planet. If not for man-made climate change, maybe the mummy would have never been uncovered. Maybe Amy's nightmare would never have awakened. But what could she do to fix things? Dr. Malam had the final say in the report. She felt helpless.

Corruptor...

Of course—Senator Jenkins. The man behind this whole mess. He'd arranged the bogus study to appease his lobbyists from the oil companies. If Amy wanted to fix things, she needed to go to the source. Prove Jenkins was taking bribes; get him thrown off the climate committee. Do some lobbying of her own. Whatever it took to make sure nothing like that hideous mummy was ever unearthed again.

She recalled the sounds outside her yurt, and the words she'd heard there. No—not heard. *Felt.* The words weren't a voice; they were a sensation in her head. But they'd amounted to a simple phrase: *Sacrifice... spoiled.*

However many thousands of years ago, a tribe had sacrificed their sorcerer to the God of Frost and Madness. His body was intended to remain in the ice forever. And now it had been exposed; it was spoiled. Pahnukh was angry.

Amy shook the thoughts away. Gods? Sorcerers? Ancient sacrifices? She was losing her mind. She needed to get off of Greenland.

She went to the airline's desk and booked the next flight to America.

———

It was a long day of travel. A brief stop in Iceland, followed by a six-hour flight to New York. Amy drifted in and out of sleep throughout. No more nightmares, but both planes felt frigid whenever she woke up. She wondered if anyone else noticed.

When she deplaned at JFK that night, she didn't head to baggage claim. She just went to the windows overlooking the tarmac and collapsed on a chair, relieved to finally be home. Everything seemed so silly now. Like it was all a dream. Had she even found a mummy in the snow? There'd been no evidence of it the next day. Amy was a scientist—evidence mattered. Maybe Dr. Malam had been right; maybe she'd just needed a break.

Through the window, commotion on the ground caught Amy's eye. The yellow-vested baggage handlers were running from the plane, casting frightened glances over their shoulders. One of them tripped. Amy was far beyond earshot, but she could still recognize the fallen woman's horrified scream as she stared wide-eyed at the baggage ramp.

Among the descending luggage, a nightmare crawled down.

It tumbled off the side and fell to the tarmac: a gaunt, naked creature, with skin the mottled orange-black of burnt sugar. It regained its footing and lumbered over to the screaming woman. A length of sharp metal gleamed in its hand.

Another baggage handler came back for the woman. He helped her up, but her foot hung at a twisted angle. The shambling creature closed the distance. The man put himself in the way.

A flash of steel drew a spray of red mist, hanging in the air like a malevolent god's frosty breath. The man clutched his throat and fell to the ground. Blood anointed Chef Johnny's whalebone knife, dripping in the mummy's hand. The risen corpse stood over its victim as the terrified woman hobbled away.

Kneeling, the mummy dipped its knife into the growing red puddle. It drew on the tarmac shapes Amy had seen in a dream.

The mummy rose. It turned its noseless face up to Amy, somehow watching with skin-sealed eyes. She felt a familiar cold grip her brain, like a tiny hand in her skull closing into a fist. A word manifested.

Vengeance.

Amy saw the mummy's mission in her mind—and from her mind, it drew the information it needed. The mummy turned and shambled away, knife in hand.

It headed southwest, on a long journey toward Capitol Hill.

BY THE WORLD FORGOT

MIA DALIA

They begin with memories. A clean mind is an easily preserved one.

Through the large glass window separating the room I am in from the one you're in, I get to watch the process I hardly understand.

My sweaty hands are worrying the brochure I was given. Everything is explained within its glossy pages. There are even helpful diagrams. I've read it several times, almost back-to-back, but it doesn't seem to provide enough of an explanation. All the words make sense, but their sum total comes up short. Perhaps there are simply no words to adequately explain how a person you love most and know best in the world can be emptied out so completely and preserved in time like some antiquity.

I remember when we first heard about the process. We were sitting across the table from each other in the breakfast nook of our home. Between us there were pancakes, scrambled eggs, a jar of honey, a bowl of mixed berries, and two mugs of coffee. The morning sun streaming through the kitchen window illuminated everything golden.

Between us there was nothing but love. Decades together had erased all distance. We had been found, learned, and loved by each other unreservedly.

There was a newspaper beside your plate—a charmingly anachronistic affectation. You licked a stray drop of honey off your finger, wiped your hands with a napkin, and handed me the newspaper, folded carefully to a specific article.

"Would you look at that?" you said, marvel rivaling with quiet disdain in your voice. "I was reading it earlier. *The latest and greatest modern invention.*"

You didn't think much of modern inventions, keeping up on them mainly just to scorn them. And there had been so many lately. Technology, everyone agreed, was entering its latest boom phase.

I took the newspaper and scanned the article.

"Oh, yes." I nodded in recognition. "Zoe was talking about it at work. Apparently, her sister is considering it."

You put down your fork. Your face changed as if the last sip of your coffee had suddenly turned sour in your mouth.

"She is? But… How? Why? I mean, they can call it whatever they like, but it's basically modern-day mummification."

"It's not that different from cryogenics, is it?" I asked, playing the devil's advocate.

"No, no, no." You shook your head vehemently. "It's very different. Cryogenics are meant to preserve the person as they are—intact. This thing is… something else entirely."

I knew enough of the basics to agree and let it drop, but you seemed interested in discussing it further.

"Why does she want to do it?" you asked. "Zoe's sister, I mean."

I shrugged. Zoe was only a work friend; her family was a mystery I had no interest in unraveling.

"Why do you think anyone might?"

"I don't know," I said. "Why does anyone get nose piercings? People are unfathomable."

"But this—" you nodded to the paper "—this is so… comprehensive. They can take everything out of you: memories, preferences, desires. And then they store it all separately and preserve you for some unknown future."

"From what I understand the idea is that they'll put it back later. Or at least, they *can* put it back in if requested."

"And if not requested? Or if it can't go back somehow? What then?"

I chased down the last raspberry with my fork and plopped it in my mouth. Its tart sweetness flooded my taste buds.

"Then I suppose a person gets a truly fresh start," I mused offhandedly.

"But it wouldn't be the same person," you mumbled quietly, "would it?"

—

You were never a proponent of technological advances, always noting their detrimental effects on our humanity. I used to call you a Luddite jokingly, but it wasn't far off the mark. You would have been happier in a less digital, more tangible world. But it was gone. The old world was nothing but a rapidly disappearing sight in the rearview mirror of the bullet train of modernity.

I knew it made you unhappy but never quite realized how much.

It got worse after your second book tanked. "Too weighty," said the reviews, and they weren't referring to the page count. "Too dour." People wanted bright, happy, feel-good stories.

You tried with your next one. I could tell you hated writing it. How strange it must have been to sit at your desk and work at it, day after day, page after page, pouring out your soul and then twisting it into something cheerful and strange and sellable.

In the end, it didn't work either. "Still too smart," seemed to be the consensus at its most generous. "Pretentiously convoluted," the uglier reviews said. "Mired in moral complexities." You had still managed to eschew formulas enough to confuse the formulaic readership.

"The writer has airs," was the one criticism you bitterly quoted more often than others. "Well, not for long," you'd grumble. "Not with all these knuckle-draggers squeezing it out of me."

Though usually so self-contained, you railed against the misconceptions of your work at a rare signing event you'd been given. It was a private conversation, but someone had recorded it with one of their wearables and posted it online.

The snowball of it turned into an avalanche quickly enough. Your career, already teetering, was cut down at the knees. Your literary agent dropped you. The university where you taught reduced your hours drastically enough to qualify as tacit firing.

And then all the noise had died down as suddenly as it began. The ensuing silence was a terrible thing.

You drank, joked at the cliché of it, and then drank some more. You reminisced about the good old days, disconnecting further and further from the world around us.

I thought it was just a phase.

I was wrong.

Using a meteorological metaphor, your unhappiness wasn't a random downpour, which presupposed an ending and then emerging sunshine. It was more of a steady drizzle and never-ending gray skies and the kind of dampness that seeps into your bones.

Like most private obsessions, it seemed to have found a focus with Neo-Mum as it had become colloquially known.

You learned all there was to know about it and would relate it to me frequently. There were different levels to the process, each with its unique degree of intensity. The overall purpose remained the same: preservation. Each person got to decide how much of themselves to preserve.

In ancient Egypt, they had it easy; less technology resulted in fewer options. They carefully removed the organs from the body and placed them in canopic jars. The body was cleaned, oiled, wrapped, and entombed, perfectly intact and ready for the next life.

In the present-day United States, mummification kept the principles of the process, morphing the rest into something hip and current like a fresh start. It was marketed as such, anyway. Aggressively so.

The crucial difference was that now the person didn't have to die. They were merely emptied out and stored for a later date. It was shocking how many people were signing up.

You followed their accounts diligently with what I had first thought was morbid curiosity. Only later did I realize that you were doing research.

You had always been a very logical person, but logic is a curiously malleable thing. Once you convince yourself of the merits of something, it adjusts to suit the new parameters.

I should have known. I should have seen the signs. In retrospect, they were glaring at me in bright neon. At the time, I was just… well, mostly busy. Being the sole breadwinner took over being your cheerleader. I let you slip into the abyss of your mind, hoping you'd reemerge eventually. For a while, it genuinely seemed like you would, though I suppose your affability in the evenings was a performance for my sake.

———

There is a certain badge of honor to a hermit lifestyle, especially for writers. Thanks, Thoreau. But I see now, my vision unblurred by the wisdom of retrospect, that one's mind is no place to dwell in alone. People need other people; hell, even other technology, to stay tethered to this world in all of its imperfections. Because the alternative is unsupportable, liable to take you to the darkest, most difficult to return from places.

I didn't realize it at the time, but now looking at you through the glass, in this sterile white room, I see clearly where we went wrong. You can love with all you've got and still let things slip through your fingers. Doesn't that just break your heart?

Too tired. That was the gist of your explanation, although you were much more eloquent about it. Tired was what I heard. Too tired of trying and failing to belong in a world that didn't make sense. Too tired of fighting the sadness that followed you around like a great weight. Too tired of disappointment and failure.

You quoted that Alexander Pope poem like a chant, like it was supposed to explain everything.

"Eternal Sunshine of the Spotless Mind." I had thought it was just an old movie.

"That's what this Neo-Mum is offering, don't you see?" you'd say. "I get it now. The world forgetting, by the world forgot."

"But that's about a lost love, isn't it? The poem and the movie both. And I'm right here, next to you," I'd counter, indignant.

You'd bite your lip, holding back words. Now I know what they were, I understand. It wasn't me you didn't love or feel loved by, it was the world itself.

"I just need a break from it all," you'd tell me, and in the end, I stopped fighting you on it. Was that a mistake?

—

Love is a strange beast. We love as we are and think it to be all-powerful, but what if it isn't enough? What if making the other person happy requires something antithetical to loving them? What if you have to let them go?

"It won't be for long," you promised. "I just need some time. It's nothing to do with you, nothing you did or didn't do. It's me. All me. I don't want to be the person I am right now, not for me and not for you. I think I just need… a reset."

I could have argued until we were both blue in the face. I could have said that I had chosen you, this version of you, and wanted nothing else. But by then, small creeping doubts had begun finding their way in, whispering that perhaps this was for the best. Perhaps it was nothing but a spring cleaning for the mind, and you'd be happier afterward.

It's hard to love an unhappy person. Especially when the ghost of the happier past lingers around the edges. A memory or two isn't too high of a cost to restore the balance, is it? After all, we are so much more than our memories.

We can justify anything when we put our minds to it. I suppose it's a survival trait.

—

I press so close to the window separating us that I can smell the lingering scent of a glass cleaner, lemony and astringent. Is it too late to admit I was wrong?

Human memories are stored in different parts of the brain. Explicit memories, which cover the events that happened to you (episodic) and general information and facts (semantic), reside in the hippocampus, the neocortex, and the amygdala. Implicit memories, pertaining to motor ability and control, are in the basal ganglia and cerebellum. And short-term working memory is the business of the prefrontal cortex.

I've learned that from the brochure clutched in my hands. It also contains a handy diagram, featuring a genderless shaved skull, one part of which is removed to show different brain parts and their names. They are distinguished by bright primary colors against the beige-gray brain matter. It looks like some futuristic entree. Spaghetti à la something.

The only person who would find this observation funny is currently undergoing a modernized mummification in the next room. Afterward, perhaps my joke would land on deaf ears.

I am not sure which part of the brain stores humor. The brochure omits any mention of it.

I wonder if this is a form of suicide. Does it count if you only kill parts of yourself?

Slowly, I watch people in white remove your memories. Even the ones with me in them. I am becoming a stranger to you, while you remain the person I know best.

I know you have a plan, a comprehensive one. Neo-Mum is big on plans and contingencies. After the body has rested and the mind has recovered from the procedure, selected memories are reintroduced. The person is reanimated to a new—*happier*—life.

Ancient Egyptians saved themselves for the afterlife. Our era is more concerned with immediacy. Everyone wants paradise here and now.

Egyptian mummies were meant to be reassembled precisely and entirely to be reanimated. Our technology is sophisticated enough to allow the à la carte approach.

———

I wonder what will happen with your unwanted memories and desires. The brochure says they are recycled, but how does it work? What can a machine do with the desire to tell stories or a passion for word games or recollections of holidays spent doing nothing but blissfully overeating to TV?

How does it reassemble what's left to complete a person? Can reconstructed love survive? You used to hate it when a jigsaw puzzle would miss a piece.

My breath draws a cloud on the glass between us. For a moment, you and the people working on you are obscured. I can imagine whatever I like. But I don't like anything my brain conjures up, so I wipe the cloud away with my sleeve.

There you are. All of you. Some of you. I press my hand against the glass and keep it there. Someone will have to wipe off my palmprint later, using that same lemony cleaning solution.

My mind clings to the words. That's it. That's what they should call this procedure: a cleaning solution. For when the world gets your mind all dirty.

My stomach growls. You were told not to eat before coming, and I fasted with you, wondering if that was our last time being on the same page. Now I'm hungry. Are you hungry too? Can hunger be removed?

You used to write, read, love with a kind of hunger, like you wanted to gobble up the entire world. It was electrifying. Where does that go now? I wonder as I study the deftly moving gloved hands working in the other room.

There's always all this talk about technology outpacing humanity. What will become of us? I suppose all we can do is wait and see.

———

The procedure appears to be finished.

I watch a stainless-steel tray being taken away and imagine it full of memories—our first date interrupted by rain, singing off-key to the radio on a cross country road trip, your first book reading, the way your hand shook signing autographs, us in Paris drunk on top of the Eiffel Tower, celebrating your first translated release, our wedding dresses of softest silk, vows exchanged in front of the bemused justice of peace, dancing outside at the 80s tribute concert, lunch sandwiches with carefully cut-off crusts and sweet notes written in marker on the plastic baggies, inadvertently getting high on floor polish fumes in our new house, digging splinters out of each other's feet because we hated carpets, years and years of unwrapped gifts, butchered songs, overanalyzed movies, nature walks, and shared meals—rendered as storable files.

This is progress. A life perfectly preserved. A person mummified. This is what we have become.

The rest of the procedure is of a corporeal nature. Somewhere in the brochure they cover what is done to the body to keep it preserved. I've skipped that part.

They let me see you afterward. You look perfectly peaceful. The goal of mummification throughout history was to keep the body lifelike and prepared for what's next. You seem ready, poised to wake up at any moment.

What happens next isn't in the brochure. Selecting memories for the next incarnation of oneself is a private process. You worked on your directives carefully, but I do not know what they are. Much like the plots of the stories you wrote, they remain a mystery to be revealed at a later time, upon completion.

You will be kept here for a previously agreed-upon period of time and then restored. That much I know. I will be able to visit you—well, your body—at any time within reason.

I can terminate all contact if I so choose. Legally, I can even divorce you, though it is still a relatively gray area.

You had qualified for a grant to undergo the procedure, something from an arts fund. It used to be a place that gave out money to aspiring writers, nourishing their hopes and dreams, but now it offers this. "A kindness," you said, "all things considered."

That means financially we're in the clear. I hate how much that motivated your decision. But I've seen your royalty checks and despaired with you, so I get it.

I am told to say my goodbyes for now, which I do, hoping you are as peaceful as you look. Wherever you are.

Your mummified body is wheeled away, though I imagine you could have floated, given half a chance, freed at last of all that you believed held you down.

What sarcophagus will they keep you in? What dreams will you dream until you are awakened?

"See you in the next life," I tell you.

There remains so much we don't know about what makes us *us*. It is a mystery as enduring as love. Still clutching the brochure, I walk out of the facility and into the blinding sunlight.

ABOUT THE AUTHORS

Meg Candelaria writes science fiction, fantasy, and horror. Her work has been published in *Daily Science Fiction, Beyond the Shadows, LOLcraft*, and other venues.

Mia Dalia is an internationally published, CWA-nominated author of all things fantastic, thrilling, scary, and strange. Her short stories of horror, noir, science fiction, mystery, crime, humor, and more have been featured in a variety of anthologies, magazines, literary journals, online, and adapted for narrative podcasts.

Her work has been voted top ten of *Tales to Terrify* 2023 and shortlisted for the CWA's Daggers Awards 2024.

She is the author of the novels *Estate Sale* and *Haven*, novellas *Tell Me a Story, Discordant, Arrokoth, Do You Know The Muffin Man?* and the collection *Smile So Red and Other Tales of Madness.*

Her upcoming work will be featured by PS Publishing, Crystal Lake Publishing, Dark Matter INK, Absinthe Press, Earthling Publications, *Ellery Queen's Mystery Magazine,* and more.

Life-long New Englander **Kristin Dearborn** was destined to write about anything that screams, squelches, or bleeds. Her first literary love was Michael Crichton. Her second, Stephen King. Dearborn earned her M.F.A. in Writing Popular Fiction from Seton Hill University and has been on the horror scene since 2010. Recent works include short stories "Ursa Diruo" in *The Rack,* "Ghosted" in *Wicked Abandoned,* and novels *Faith of Dawn* (2024) *Downlines* (2023) *The Amazing Alligator Girl* (2022). When not writing, Kristin enjoys hiking the northeast, traveling, and hanging out with her pets. Her cat, Ash, offered his (many) opinions on "One Hundred Dead Cats."

Ray DeChant is a professional wrangler of teens and an alumnus of Mary Robinette Kowal's Short Story Cohort, with one previous publication in *Mslexia Magazine.* When she's not working or writing, she knits socks, runs slowly, and cooks too much soup.

Christopher La Vigna is a horror author whose stories and poems have appeared in anthologies such as *Horrorscope Vol.3, Strangest Fiction Volume 2, Violent Advents,* and *That Old House: The Bathroom Volume 1.* He can be found on Bluesky @chrislavigna.bsky.social, and on Instagram @instant_insanity_productions. He currently resides in Yonkers with his wife Jessica.

Carter Lappin (she/her) is a Californian author. Her works of fiction have appeared in publications such as Brigid's Gate Press, Manawaker Studio, Timber Ghost Press, and Air and Nothingness Press. You can find her on Twitter/X at @CarterLappin.

Jennifer Lesh Fleck is an emerging dark fiction writer with stories published or upcoming in *MetaStellar, Gamut, If There's Anyone Left, Heartlines Spec, Cosmic Horror Monthly, Flash Fiction Online*, and the 2023 Shirley Jackson Award winner for best anthology, among others. She lives with her family near Portland, Oregon in a home that's a dead ringer for the Amityville Horror House, though repainted a cheery jade green. She's a grateful recipient of the 2025 Superstars Expanding Universe scholarship, and her work is often informed by the challenges of lifelong hidden disability from a rare inherited disorder.

Find her @mettle.and.metal (Instagram), @jen_lesh_fleck (X), and jenniferleshfleck.com.

Stewart Moore has had short fiction published in anthologies edited by Ellen Datlow (2010) and Paula Guran (2011), and published by Air and Nothingness Press (2022) and Flame Tree Publishing (2024); in the magazines *Mysterion* (2018), *Diabolical Plots* (2019) and *Lady Churchill's Rosebud Wristlet* (2020); and in the podcast *Pseudopod* (2020). He also wrote the nonfiction book *Jewish Ethnic Identity and Relations in Hellenistic Egypt: With Walls of Iron?* (2015).

Ute Orgassa was born and raised in Germany. She now lives with her family in the Bay Area. Her short stories have been published by Shortwave Publishing, Haunted Words Press, *Alternative Milk Magazine*, Punk Noir, Alien Buddha Press, and Infested Publishing.

Her play *A Different Track* was produced by Awkward Pigeons Theater.

José Raposo Santos writes strange stories. Hailing from Portugal, his work has featured in *Archive of the Odd #1*, *Lunatics Radio Hour* podcast, *Escalators to Hell: Shopping Mall Horrors*, and other such publications.

Find the author online as CCskeleton or Customer Care Skeleton.

Research for this story included reading the article "Aztecs on Mercy" by Mi Ainsel, and more. The author suggests visiting mexicolore.co.uk/Aztecs for those interested.

Zach Shephard's fiction has appeared in places like *Fantasy & Science Fiction*, *Flash Fiction Online*, and Flame Tree Publishing's *Haunted House Short Stories* anthology. For more of his work, check out zachshephard.com.

B.F. Vega is a horror writer, political poet, and over-worked theater artist living in the North Bay Area of California. A member of the HWA, her short stories and poetry have appeared in numerous anthologies and magazines, including: *Dark Nature, Dark Cheer: Cryptids Emerging, Haunts & Hellions, Good Southern Witches*, and *Club Chicxclub*, among others. Most recently, her horror western "OWLS" appeared in *Zehlreg Augustus Grindstone's Spectacular Western Oddity Emporium*. She

is still shocked when people refer to her as an author—
every time.

Morgan West-Burnham is currently a student in
Western Colorado University's Creative Writing MFA
Program. She has a short story in the anthology *Chaotic
Cupids* published by WordFire Press. When she's not
writing speculative fiction, she works as a middle school
English teacher.

ABOUT THE EDITOR(S)

A.C. Bauer is the founder and editor-in-chief of Cat Eye Press. He's been a writer as long as he can remember, and his love of the horror genre runs deep. He grew up on classic 90s slashers like *Scream* and *I Know What You Did Last Summer* and read a ton of *Goosebumps* books. You can learn more about him at acbauerwrites.com.

Frankie the Cat is the fiendish feline mascot of Cat Eye Press and self-proclaimed "brains behind the operation." He's part demon, part shapeshifting imaginary friend, part cat(?), and a total horror enthusiast. He loves exploring the darkest corners of the imagination and seeing what new directions his favorite genre goes. In his spare time, Frankie likes to play internet poker and take long walks on the beach.

CONTENT WARNINGS

"Bound by Love" by Stewart Moore:
Terminal illness (cancer), death, graphic descriptions
of embalming

"Going Home" by Ute Orgassa:
Implied death

"Our Hearts a Hecatomb" by J.R. Santos:
Blood, death, violence

"Dead Kings, No Crowns" by Christopher La Vigna:
Drugs, violence

"#Rich-Tok" by B.F. Vega:
Blood, gore, death, murder

"One Hundred Dead Cats" by Kristin Dearborn:
Whimsical cat on undead cat violence

"Reanimation" by Carter Lappin:
Death, shooting

"Painted As a Villain" by Morgan West-Burnham:
Dead and desecrated cats

"In My Little, Dead Way" by Jennifer Lesh Fleck:
Terminal illness, death

"Rot" by Ray DeChant:
Violence, Orientalism

"The Telltale LVAD" by Meg Candelaria:
Body horror

"Servants of Frost and Madness" by Zach Shephard:
Blood, body horror, death, mentions of climate change

"By The World Forgot" by Mia Dalia:
Themes and mention of suicide

HUNGRY FOR MORE HORROR?

Taste the dark deliciousness of

CURSED COOKING

a hybrid horror anthology/cookbook.
It's a smorgasbord of scares!

AVAILABLE NOW AT CATEYEPRESS.COM